Guardian Angel

By Anthea Cohen

GUARDIAN ANGEL
ANGEL OF DEATH
ANGEL OF VENGEANCE
ANGEL WITHOUT MERCY

Guardian Angel

ANTHEA COHEN

PUBLISHED FOR THE CRIME CLUB BY
DOUBLEDAY & COMPANY, INC.
GARDEN CITY, NEW YORK
1985

All of the characters in this book
are fictitious, and any resemblance
to actual persons, living or dead,
is purely coincidental.

Library of Congress Cataloging in Publication Data

Cohen, Anthea.
Guardian angel.

I. Title.
PR6053.O34G8   1985   823'.914   84-13771
ISBN 0-385-19871-X

Copyright © 1985 by Anthea Cohen
All Rights Reserved
Printed in the United States of America
First Edition in the United States of America

Guardian Angel

CHAPTER 1

Jack Sampson, Greyfriars' head porter, pushed the trolley of sterile disposables through the swing-doors.

"Special delivery, just for you, Sister," he said. "Derek is away so you wouldn't have got these for ages unless I'd brought them up."

Carmichael did not respond. She disliked Sampson and was suspicious immediately of his friendly overture. She was right to be suspicious, for Sampson left the trolley, went over and leaned against her office door. He was a small man, and his navy uniform jacket gave out a sickly smell of dried sweat. His sparse, greasy black hair was slicked back above his ferret-like face.

"Do you want me for something?" Carmichael asked coldly. She remained seated at her desk and did not look up.

"Well, as a matter of fact, I wanted to ask you a favour. Like, if you could see your way . . ." This remark did make Carmichael raise her eyes to his. They were small, brown, and partially masked by tinted glasses.

"A favour? What can I do for you, Mr. Sampson?" Carmichael asked.

He came a little farther into the office and bent over her confidentially.

"It's the wife. She's on the operating list, on the waiting list, to have her knee done. She goes out and does a bit of cleaning and, well, she can hardly do it now with her knee as it is, so I wondered if you could have a word with Mr. Dalby and get her put up the list a bit. After all, she's hospital—well, not hospital staff, but related." He looked at her, his eyes narrowing a little as if he half-expected the reply he got.

"Have a word with Mr. Dalby? No, I did not know your wife was on the waiting list. I'm not in the habit of seeing the list. It is entirely the secretary's and the Consultant's job to deal with that, it is nothing to do with me. Why should I speak to Mr. Dalby? When her turn comes she will be called in as soon as we have a bed available."

Sampson, obviously making an effort to keep his temper, tried again.

"Well, I know that, Sister, but you know what I mean, a word in the right place . . . and you do see Mr. Dalby all the time . . . You could mention—the wife of the head porter, you know. You could do your best for me, couldn't you? I mean, I'd make it right with you. Well, like today, sterile supplies aren't going to be delivered for another couple of hours, and if you were short . . . See what I mean? You scratch my back and I'll scratch yours."

"I know nothing of the kind, Mr. Sampson. If we're short of portering staff, then I must take my late deliveries with the rest, though I think it is largely due to mismanagement. Please don't expect me to do anything at all. I'm sorry about your wife, but there are plenty of others in the same predicament. You know what the waiting list is like."

Sampson did lose his temper then, and his face twisted into an ugly scowl.

"Oh, thanks," he said bitterly, "thanks for nothing. Now if she was private and you mentioned to old Dalby that she was going to pay, don't you worry she'd be in in a flash on the private floor. That's how it's done, isn't it? It makes me sick. There shouldn't be a private ward. To be able to be put out of pain because you've got money, it's all wrong and I don't agree with it. Nor do I agree with the surgeons raking it in like that. I know the fees they charge."

Carmichael stood up. "I'm sure you think so, Mr. Sampson, but I'd rather not talk about it further, if you don't mind. That is the province of the surgeons. They do their best. It's hard enough with the waiting lists, such as they are. I'm sorry, but I will not discuss this further."

"No, I know you won't, but you could do something if she was paying . . . Oh, I know, I know this set-up, don't worry. Old Dalby, he makes a nice little bit, specially out of a hip. I've seen 'em, scratching together their money to go private, and some of them do have to scratch. I even know one of 'em, poor bugger."

"Don't dare speak about Mr. Dalby like that," said Carmichael, her sharp nose twitching, her face flushed. "Your views on private work and, indeed, your political views are well known, Mr. Sampson. I would be grateful if you would refrain from trying to seduce my nurses away from the College of Nursing into joining your union. That is all I have to say. I have work to do if you haven't."

Indignation had made her rise and now she sat down again at her desk. She pulled some notes towards her and did not look up.

Sampson stood there for a moment silently, obviously trying to think of a parting shot. He found one:

"I'll do what I damn well like about the union. Some of these poor kids would be better belonging to it. Look at the way nurses are exploited just because they won't leave their patients. Oh, I know what goes on there too, the bloody College. They do nothing by the look of it. They'll agree to anything. The College is a wash-out. I shall make as many nurses as I can leave and come into something worthwhile. The College . . . and it's 'A nurse can't strike.' Why can't she? Everyone else does."

"Yes, in your type of union. You have absolutely no sense of service. The nurses don't feel like that and I hope they will not be misled by people like you. If I do what you want me to do, I can have my linen more promptly, or my surgical stores or my kitchen stores. No, thanks, I don't work in that way, Mr. Sampson. Will you please unload the trolley and leave."

"Oh no, it won't get unloaded here. It'll go down to the women's surgical and you can wait for yours, Sister Carmichael, if that's how you feel. I only asked you a favour and you're not getting anything from me if you don't bloody well do anything in return."

He left her office, took hold of the trolley handle, backed it through the swing-doors again, and was gone.

Staff Nurse Minter came up to Carmichael's office.

"Phew, does that man stink! Even his best friend . . . Not that he's got any. Did you have a spat with him, Sister? Better not to, you know what he's like."

"Yes, I know what he's like, and it's my business what I say to porters. Please get on with your work, Staff Nurse Minter," Carmichael snapped.

"All right, Sister, I was only just mentioning it," said Minter, smiling a little as she walked away.

"Bring me the air freshener, Staff Nurse," Carmichael called after her.

Minter grinned more broadly and went to get it.

Carmichael had recently been transferred from Casualty at her own request when a vacancy had occurred to take over the orthopaedic ward. She thought that after three years in Casualty she was losing touch with the patients and, if she wanted promotion, she must be familiar with all branches of nursing.

While she was in Casualty, ambition had surged in her again —after her nervous breakdown and sojourn in the psychiatric hospital and subsequent fight back to health. She now felt she must regain a post similar to the one she had held in St. Matthews Hospital, that of Nursing Officer, and she thought this move to the orthopaedic ward was a step in the right direction.

She was now Sister of Gatcombe and Calbourne wards, male and female orthopaedic. Each ward held twenty-two beds. In the space between the wards was Carmichael's office, a fair-sized ward kitchen, a clinic room, and sluice rooms. For a hospital that was not so young and had had many alterations, Greyfriars was a satisfactory hospital for Carmichael. She had known that the moment she had entered it. It was the right size, a hundred and thirty beds, situated in a small town that she liked and found comfortable to live in. She looked round her domain with satisfaction, the irritation brought by

Jack Sampson gradually fading away with the smell of his perspiration. She turned for a moment and gazed out of the window behind her. The orthopaedic wards were on the fourth floor with only the theatres above them, and she liked even the position of her wards. The irritation evaporated completely and she gave her thoughts to the morning ahead.

CHAPTER 2

Tuesday was an important day: it was the morning of Mr. Dalby's orthopaedic round. This started promptly at nine-thirty and was more majestic than the rounds done by the other orthopaedic consultant, Mr. Parsons. Mr. Dalby came with a large entourage and expected—Carmichael bridled at the thought—special service from the Sister, and this he got. Carmichael was convinced that she was more efficient than her predecessor.

She went round both wards, checking that they were tidy, that no newspapers were on the floor, that no one was secretly smoking, that the windows were open the required amount—Mr. Dalby liked fresh air—also checking that the various leg extensions, plasters, splints, and weights were all in order. She walked round telling a nurse here and a nurse there: "Straighten that bed," "Take that urinal off the locker," "Put away that pair of slippers." Then she heard the Consultant and his followers coming up the stairs.

Carmichael stood at the ward door trying to combine an air of deference and friendliness that would let her nurses see that she was not like the other Sisters—indeed, had a different, closer relationship with the Consultant. She stood there as the steps grew louder on the stairs, a nurse beside her with the note trolley ready to hand each person's notes to Carmichael as the great man arrived at each patient's bed.

Mr. Edwin Dalby did not use the lift. He preferred to walk up the stairs, saying it was good exercise. The house officer, who had been working nearly all night and who had twisted his ankle, indicated behind the surgeon's back that he did not agree with him, but this morning he knew better than to say anything directly to his chief. Everything was not quite as Mr. Dalby wished this morning. First, the secretary, clutching her clipboard, had been five minutes late and he had had to wait in the front hall for her to join them. He had not said much, just glanced at his watch and murmured:

"Something hold you up, Miss Smith?"

She had not answered, for at that moment his house officer, Dr. Manning, also tardy, had rushed along the corridor, a none-too-clean white coat flying open, his stethoscope still round his neck, arriving almost with a skid beside him.

"Sorry, sir, got held up," he said, panting slightly. He was an untidy young man.

Mr. Dalby's registrar, Mr. Harris, was standing behind him, a look of patient nobility on his face. He was always on time, always in a clean white coat, always correct, and for some reason Mr. Dalby disliked him much more than he did his house officer. He did not, however, bother to analyse his feelings, but he did look with some distaste at his house officer, and again said nothing about the coat or the lateness. Behind him was the physiotherapist, white-coated, also holding a clipboard, waiting to take down Mr. Dalby's wishes. They ascended the stairs, the Consultant first, then the secretary, the physiotherapist, the registrar, and the house officer, panting and limping slightly. They arrived at the orthopaedic ward's door and Mr. Dalby greeted Carmichael.

"Good morning, Sister. Everything ready for me, I hope?"

"Of course, sir."

Carmichael refused to call Mr. Dalby by his name as the other Sisters did. She felt, although he was comparatively young, he was the type of man who would appreciate the old-fashioned "sir," and she was right. Mr. Dalby nodded pleasantly and walked into the ward. Disaster struck early.

In the first bed was a young man who had had his knee operated on and was due to go home. Carmichael had put him into bed because she thought it made the ward look tidier, but Mr. Dalby objected.

"Why is this man in bed? Surely he is going home the day

after tomorrow?" He flicked the notes in his hand and the registrar stepped forward eagerly.

"Yes indeed, sir, I'm hoping so." He nodded to the patient and the patient nodded back watchfully, obviously wondering if they were going to change the date.

"Get him up, Sister, he's no need to be in bed."

Carmichael flushed but said nothing.

At the next bed was Mr. Jennings, his leg up on extension, the weights at the end of the bed heavy. He did not look particularly well. He gazed at Mr. Dalby with apathy, knowing that there was no chance of his going home yet—a road traffic accident had seen to that.

"Good morning, Mr. er—Mr. Dixon." Mr. Dalby glanced at the notes that had been put into his hand.

"I'm not Mr. Dixon, I'm Mr. Jennings," said the patient, affronted as they always were when such a mistake occurred.

Mr. Dalby turned a cold eye on the nurse who was handing out the notes.

"Why have you given me the wrong notes? Why have you handed the wrong notes to Sister?" he asked.

"Oh, I'm terribly sorry, sir, I thought . . ." The little nurse followed her Sister's example in calling him sir, but it did nothing to mollify him. He turned to Carmichael.

"Please be more careful, Sister, and check the notes before you give them to me. I can hardly be expected . . ." He tailed off as the right notes were handed to him.

Sister Carmichael flushed even redder and cast a furious glance at the nurse, who knew she would hear more about this incident later. For the moment the nurse's concentration had gone—she had been thinking of her boy-friend, with whom she'd had a crashing row the night before, but she knew she'd have to watch it.

The rest of the round proceeded almost without incident. There was just a slight disagreement between the house officer and Mr. Dalby and another one between the physiotherapist and the registrar. The physiotherapist could well hold her own. She knew that her breed was very thin on the ground, and with a word from the orthopaedic surgeon she would say:

"Well, I'm sorry, Mr. Dalby, we just won't be able to cover it. We haven't got the staff." There was a certain amount of truth in this, so if reproof came her way it was covered with a sugar coating.

"Well, do your best, Miss Mortimer."

As they walked out of the ward, having finished the round, Mr. Harris, the registrar, and the Consultant were talking quietly, and Mr. Harris drew a notebook from his pocket and pointed to a list.

Carmichael drew near. She didn't want to miss anything, particularly something that might concern her patients.

"Yes, I see what you mean. Well, there's the knee going home and the other chap with the dislocated shoulder can go, he seems satisfactory and if it dislocates again, well . . . that'll make two beds. Then in the women's ward there's that Mrs. . . . what's her name? She could be transferred, couldn't she? I mean, she's taking up a bed and she's going to be in for some time unless we do something about it. Oh, I know her relatives apparently don't want to know . . ." He glanced towards the medical social worker who had joined them. She nodded.

"I'll see what I can do—about the relatives, I mean." Mr. Dalby nodded graciously.

"Can I get two hips in then, sir? The waiting list . . ." the registrar went on.

"Yes, you can, but you've got to leave something for emergencies." Again Dalby sounded irritable. The bed question always made him scratchy, the waiting list even scratchier.

The round was finished. Carmichael did not want to be summarily dismissed in front of her nurses; she wanted a pleasant "Thank you, Sister" from the Consultant. She was cross with Mr. Harris for diverting his attention; she wanted to be spoken to about her patients, the way they were being treated, her handling of the ward. As the nurses walked by they would notice. Carmichael thought a great deal about the impression she made on her nurses and, indeed, on everyone else.

At that moment the swing-doors opened and Miss O'Donoghue, the Nursing Officer, came in. She should have had more sense than to come up when Mr. Dalby was doing a round, Carmichael thought. However, she could not say anything to Miss O'Donoghue, who seemed to sweep everything before her, never seeing when she was not wanted. She was a pretty girl, tall, slender, younger than Carmichael, dark short hair curling round her face, her eyes very blue. They always seemed to be twinkling with amusement.

She came in quite happily, not retiring backwards through the swing-doors as another Nursing Officer might have done or as Carmichael might have done when she was Nursing Officer. She walked forward smiling, her beautiful mouth curving seductively. Mr. Dalby gave the first wide smile of the morning.

"Oh, good morning, Miss O'Donoghue. A nice breath of Irish air to clear away the morning's problems." It was a gallant speech and Carmichael hated him for it. He said perfunctorily to Carmichael, without looking at her, his eyes still fixed on Miss O'Donoghue:

"Thank you, Sister, and try to see that Nurse can read the names of the patients next time and hand me the correct notes." Carmichael felt this was for the benefit of the Nursing Officer and she loathed Mr. Dalby at that moment. The Consultant went through the swing-doors and Carmichael heard him descending the stairs.

"Using the stairs as usual, eh?" Miss O'Donoghue laughed. "A real stickler, isn't he? Well, the house officer won't be best pleased. He had quite a morning in Casualty, I can tell you. Patel was off. They had an overdose in early and he had to cope with it. He was up about five, poor little devil, and I believe he's hurt his ankle. Still, Mr. Dalby won't worry about that, will he, Sister?"

"I really don't know. I think he's as thoughtful as anyone to his juniors," said Carmichael frostily. The Nursing Officer cast her an amused glance.

"That's right, dear, always stick up for your consultants. How's old Parsons?"

"Old Parsons, Miss O'Donoghue?" Again Carmichael's voice was cold. "I suppose you are referring to Mr. Parsons." Mr. Parsons was getting close to retirement but Carmichael still resented the word "old." Her consultants, Mr. Dalby and Mr. Parsons, she felt, were her property and must be protected. She disliked anyone saying anything against them, be it senior or junior nurse, or another doctor.

The Nursing Officer did a round with Carmichael, stopped to speak to a junior nurse as she went by hurrying to the kitchen, stopping at the bedside to talk to a patient with Carmichael standing impatiently beside her.

"Any coffee going in your office, Carmichael?" she asked when it was finished.

"No, I haven't ordered it yet, but I will if you like." Carmichael knew better than to offend the Nursing Officer. After all, it was such a post that she herself was after. Perhaps this pretty girl would not stay long unmarried. Carmichael knew she was already engaged, but of course she might not leave even if she did marry. Everyone went on working these days and it hampered promotion for those lower down the scale.

"No, don't bother, I'll have some downstairs with Sister Hamble," said Miss O'Donoghue breezily. She raised her hand in farewell, spoke to another nurse on her way out, and disappeared through the swing-doors.

Miss O'Donoghue was not, as Carmichael knew, in the habit of using the stairs. Although the lift was slow and creaky, there had not been enough money to put in a new, silent, modern one, and the old one was having to do for the moment. Carmichael listened to the clang of the gates and the slight whirr of the lift as it descended to the next floor. Surely she could have walked one flight if Mr. Dalby could walk down them all, Carmichael thought with contempt, then turned to the nurse to whom Miss O'Donoghue had spoken when she was leaving.

"Nurse East, you'd better start the dressings now, please."

The nurse nodded brightly. "O.K.," she said.

Carmichael did not agree with this. She disliked the habit of saying "O.K." and calling each other by their Christian names. No one called her Agnes—it was Sister Carmichael, she insisted on that—but there was nothing she could do to stop the other nurses. It had already become a habit.

She walked towards her office, looking at her watch as she did so. It was too late now for coffee. It had not been a satisfactory morning up till now, she thought. But still—she shrugged slightly—maybe it would get better. Mr. Parsons would come later in the day and he was easier to do a round with, she had to admit, but how she disliked Miss O'Donoghue referring to him as "old Parsons"!

The rest of the day was uneventful. There was no operating on Tuesdays, unless of course an emergency came in, but today there was none.

At five o'clock Carmichael was ready to go home, having given a meticulous report to her Staff Nurse which caused the girl to yawn furtively now and again, for most of the things Carmichael was telling her she was fully aware of. When she had finished Carmichael cast a last anxious glance round, as she always did when she was leaving her domain in someone else's charge. Then she went to the changing-room, got out of her uniform, hung it up in her locker, put on her civvies, and made for home.

CHAPTER 3

In three years Carmichael had transformed her little cottage. The garden in front was pretty, the beds full of dahlias and asters. She was glad, she thought, as she turned from her front door to look at them, that she had taken the trouble to buy so many. She had been a little dismayed at the expense but it had been worth it.

Her front door opened directly into the sitting-room. The people who visited her, Amy Jones, the children's ward Sister at her last hospital, and Mrs. Jenks, a friend, both had exclaimed with admiration at her arrangement. Dear Mrs. Jenks. Carmichael smiled benignly and wondered if she came to see her or the cats. Probably the latter, but Carmichael didn't mind. Tibbles had been cared for so often by Mrs. Jenks; Torty, a more recent addition to the family, had arrived later but was equally loved.

Inside too the cottage was transformed—chintz curtains—and she herself had papered every room. The two bedrooms upstairs, the bathroom and sitting-room, the minute dining-room and kitchen, she had done it all. Carmichael was unused to such work, but she felt she had done it very professionally, and she had enjoyed every moment.

She looked round fondly and remembered the day when she had driven along the road, remembered stopping and looking at the "For Sale" notice at the cottage gate and how she had vowed the little place would be hers. Well, I do not make promises to myself lightly, she thought. Getting the mortgage had been comparatively easy. Moving her few things from the flat sixty miles away had been expensive but all of it had been worthwhile. She had a house of her own which she meant to keep. She wasn't going to move anymore. Greyfriars was to be the last. Well, at nearly forty she felt she could look for promotion in this hospital and stay there—Nursing Officer—and from that post . . . who knows?

As usual Tibbles and Torty came bursting through the cat-flap in the back door when they heard her put the key in the lock. It didn't matter where they were, they seemed to hear her and come running. It was nice.

She busied herself getting a meal and preparing the cats' food and went on with her comfortable thoughts. Wait a minute, she said to herself almost humorously, just a minute, you haven't got the Nursing Officer's post yet, so don't start thinking of anything higher than that for the moment. But she did think about it. She would like very much to be more senior before she left. Retirement at fifty dangled before her. Carmichael had ceased to think of herself as married—she felt that with her looks marriage was not for her—but there were other things besides marriage.

She put the vegetables on to cook and took the cold meat out of her refrigerator and put it on the working surface. Then she fed Tibbles and Torty. In their separate ways they played their usual game with the meal. Tibbles walked all round hers, sniffing as if she was going to refuse it. Torty got in straight away, munching, back low on the ground, tail stretching out behind her. Tibbles then, as usual, took a long look at Torty and assumed the same position. Both cats made a gnawing noise which in the stillness of the cottage pleased Carmichael.

Opening the back door, she went into the garden. She had had her two fruit trees pruned by a man from the town and they had a much better shape now, not so straggly. The grass beneath them was cut by a boy who lived in a cottage nearby, and it was a lovely place for the cats to romp in and a nice place too for Carmichael to sit in a deck-chair on sunny days. She gazed around her appreciatively. It was better than the Nursing Home, better than the flat. She had really come a long way and she did not intend to let anything make her slip back.

Often she thought of her life so far. After all, starting in an orphanage wasn't the best of starts. Though of course she didn't know their backgrounds, she would be surprised to know that any of the other Sisters had started the way she had. She didn't tell anybody about her childhood. Then she thought, too, of the awful plunge latterly, into the psychiatric ward. But that was over now, three and a quarter years back. She might be nearly forty but still called herself, determinedly, thirty-eight.

A slight hissing noise from the kitchen sent her hurrying back to slant the lid of the vegetable saucepan and turn down the heat. Then she went into the sitting-room and poured herself a glass of sherry. Should she ask Mrs. Jenks down again? She really enjoyed having her. No, better not, it was really Jones's turn. Poor old Jones. It was nice to say that. Yes, she'd telephone her and ask her down for a week-end. It meant a lot to Jones to get away for a bit. She hadn't a lot of friends—poor old Jones.

Back in the hospital Mr. Parsons arrived to do a round. He came up in the lift, no puffing up the stairs for him. He was a fat, jovial man, his white hair rapidly thinning. He still, much to everyone's amusement, wore a gold watch chain and frequently consulted his gold hunter. This, for some reason, made the nurses laugh and he was aware of it, but because he was such an amiable man he didn't mind.

"I thought I'd make a late round, Nurse Minter." He always remembered the names of nurses, a fact which endeared him to them.

"It was Mr. Dalby's round this morning, Mr. Parsons, and you know what that's like," said Staff Nurse Minter.

Mr. Parsons laughed. "Well, they are all the same, the orthopods," he said philosophically. "I remember one I used to go round with as a houseman"—he was a great reminiscer was Parsons—"he would stop by a bed when everybody was as busy as hell and wanted to get on with their work and he'd say, 'Now what we have to consider is this, whether this lady fell because her hip broke, or fell and broke her hip.'" Staff

Nurse laughed and he continued: "An academic question, seeing the old lady was lying there with a broken hip, but I suppose it was worthy of some thought, even a little experiment, though I don't know how you'd experiment. Push the old lady down the stairs?" Mr. Parsons was sometimes sarcastic and sometimes funny but rarely unkind.

They did the round with very little ceremony. He knew all his patients' names and Staff Nurse Minter was relaxed with him. He brought out this feeling in the staff and when he departed he always left his patients feeling decidedly better than when he arrived. He took his leave of Staff Nurse, went through the swing-doors to the lift, then suddenly came back.

"Oh, by the way, had any more trouble with those yobbos?" Nurse Minter grimaced.

"Yes and no," she said. "We had a couple up the other night. They came up to see a chap who'd been brought in after crashing his motor bike. He'd been unconscious so we kept him in. They seem to think they can come whenever they want to. Still, they were pretty docile and went after Sister Carmichael had told them off."

"Good. I worry about this element. It could get worse, you know. One Casualty department I read about—probably you read it too—had a bad time with them."

Staff Nurse Minter nodded. "Yes I did. They would have smashed up the place if three porters hadn't come.

"If you have any trouble you send for a porter. Don't stand any nonsense."

"I'll try not to." Staff Nurse Minter was almost as pretty as the Nursing Officer, and Mr. Parsons smiled at her benignly.

"I can understand Sister Carmichael being able to handle it. I wouldn't like to cross her myself. Not that she's not a damn good Sister, but you know how it is, if these boys get above themselves don't try and handle it yourself. You never know, they can be rough."

Staff Nurse Minter nodded again. "I know, I meet some of them when I'm going home in my car at night after duty. I lock both doors. A policeman we had on the ward told me to do that."

"You should. It's a good idea," Mr. Parsons said. "Well, I'll come round after I've operated tomorrow."

Minter smiled at him again and this time he did not come back after he'd gone through the swing-doors. Minter heard the lift grid clang as he entered it to descend.

She went back into the ward office and sat down, nurses coming in occasionally to ask her questions. She pulled the report book towards her and filled in the few things Mr. Parsons had ordered as he walked round the ward. Minter liked being in charge. Carmichael was all right, a bit fusty though. When she was there somehow the whole place felt different, but she wasn't bad. She was a good Sister, one of the old school, though, thought the Staff Nurse. Still, her thoughts went on, she can't be all that old, forty-five perhaps? Could be a bit more. She went on writing in the report book that she would have to take later to her Nursing Officer.

CHAPTER 4

Next morning it was Miss O'Donoghue who again ruffled Carmichael's calm. The Irish girl had, as Carmichael already knew, strong views which in many ways supported those of Jack Sampson, and Carmichael suspected that the Nursing Officer was a member of his union.

"It is only the fact that they know we won't strike that has kept our salaries down all these years and, really, we haven't caught up properly now, whatever you say."

Carmichael did not agree with this—she considered the Nursing Officer's salary perfectly adequate—and retorted tartly: "Well, I'm quite sure that some of the nurses who trained in the early thirties would be astonished if they knew our salaries now."

"Yes, and they would be shocked if they saw the prices we have to pay for things now, too."

The Nursing Officer went off through the swing-doors before Carmichael was able to reply. Indeed, she did not wish to do so. She hated getting mixed up in this kind of argument, which she felt was quite irrelevant to what nursing stood for.

After the Nursing Officer had left, Carmichael calmed herself. She carefully turned the pages of the notes she was checking, noting that they were all correctly filled in and putting them into a pile near her ready to put back into the note trolley. Minter, her Staff Nurse, who had been standing near and listening to the conversation, said:

"She's right, you know, Sister. They do rely on us having what they used to call a vocation, being dedicated. They have always relied on that, so they've always managed to keep us cheap labour. Not so much now, perhaps, but there's a long history of it in nursing. I've got to say I agree with her."

"Well, I don't. I certainly wouldn't strike, whatever happened. I would not leave my patients. Never."

"Yeah, maybe, but you'd probably take the money if you got a rise because *we'd* left them," said Staff Nurse, scribbling away on a clipboard she had in her hand.

"What's that you're writing?" asked Sister Carmichael, who wished the subject to be closed.

"Oh, only just trying to remember a new procedure. I read the sheet and then forgot some of it and thought I'd better put it down and then I might remember. I'm doing it for my own benefit, before I tell the nurses, I mean."

"It seems rather a haphazard way of doing it, Staff Nurse. If you want another copy of the sheet you can have it, you know." Carmichael spoke crisply. She was still annoyed. There was far too much of this trade union business going round the hospital, far too much. She did not notice that her Staff Nurse had followed her.

"It's sheet number ten, on extension. Can I request another one, Sister?"

Carmichael turned. "Yes, Staff Nurse, but try not to lose this one. I suppose that's what you did with the last?"

"Yes, I put it down somewhere and then . . . I expect it's around but I just can't put my hand on it," said Staff Nurse Minter, the end of her pen between her teeth. She looked at Carmichael sideways. "I suppose you don't agree with Jack the porter at all, then. I don't know whether the nurses would join them. I sometimes wonder if we should."

"No, I do not agree with Jack Sampson, and I wish he wouldn't keep coming round here and inflaming the nurses. It really is too bad. He's only supposed to speak to them in their off-duty time, but I don't think he should be allowed to speak to them at all."

"Oh, come on, Sister Carmichael, free speech and all that," said her Staff Nurse as she turned round.

Carmichael made a mental note that her hair was far too

long. She'd tell her about it later. She'd either have to do it up in a bun or have it cut. She put the notes in the trolley, spoke to one or two patients, peered round a screen where a nurse was doing a dressing, watched her for a moment, nodded approval, closed the curtains, and went back into her own office.

Jack Sampson was still on Carmichael's mind. He was a bad influence, she thought, a thoroughly bad influence. She looked at her watch—lunch-time.

She took her cloak from the hook on the door and threw it round her shoulders. Carmichael always wore her cloak whether it was warm or cold. She liked the feeling it gave her; she always felt she walked better in her cloak. She left her ward and, contrary to her usual practice, got into the lift, closed the old-fashioned grille after closing the wooden doors, pressed the button, and went down to the ground floor. Normally she would have used the stairs, but she was a little late for lunch and it was rather frowned upon if the Sisters went into the dining-room and had to be waited on after the others had all been served.

In the dining-room she looked across at the Sisters' table. There were four Sisters there. She walked across and sat down and they greeted her. Sister Hill was rather like Jones, Carmichael's fat friend from the other hospital, but she was jollier-looking than Jones. She was theatre Sister.

"Brown Windsor again," she said and bent to the soup she was eating.

"Anything else as an alternative?" asked Carmichael, looking round for the menu, which appeared to be absent.

"You must be joking," said Sister Hill, and Carmichael nodded her thanks to the dining-room maid as she put down a plate of soup in front of her. She took a spoonful and before the maid had time to leave she said:

"It's cold—well, cool, anyway."

"Well, you were late, Sister," said the girl looking up at the electric clock on the wall, "seven minutes late."

"Three minutes late, no more, and anyway I should not have thought the soup would have had time to cool in that time," said Carmichael. "It must have been cool to start with. I don't imagine it was heated up properly."

The dining-room maid shrugged. It was obvious that Carmichael was not a favourite of hers. She walked back to the kitchen, her bottom twitching angrily.

"Better not cause hostility, dear," said one of the other Sisters, "she'll only give you gristly pieces of meat if you do and the soggy bits of pie." There was a general laugh at the table in which Carmichael did not join.

"What about Jack Sampson then, did he come to see you?" Sister Hill looked across the table to Sister Hamble from women's surgical.

Hamble nodded. "Yes he did. He's got a point, you know. I don't think I could do it, but I don't know. My young nurses don't feel so . . . not so against giving some kind of demonstration. I think people take us for granted, and the kids think that particularly."

"They should be glad to have a job in this economy," said Carmichael. The other Sisters all looked at her in surprise, not so much at the remark but at the bitter tone in which it was made.

"Yes, we know that, but we've all trained to become nurses and these kids are in training and it's quite a slog isn't it? Let's face it."

"Nowadays it isn't a slog at all, in my opinion," said Carmichael.

"Well, you're older than they are, Carmichael," said Hill mildly. She pushed away her soup-plate and accepted with some degree of suspicion another plate on which lay some meat with gravy surrounded by rice.

"What's that?" inquired Sister Hamble.

"Kidneys in rice, it said on the menu. I chose it because I didn't think kidneys could be tough. They're probably tinned, anyway," said Hamble, tucking in. "It's not bad."

The others were served and Carmichael had the same. She did not want to remark upon the fact that there was no menu on the table as there was supposed to be. She assumed it had been collected before she got there. She sat gazing at the food for a moment.

"It's a disgrace to nursing, the very thought of it really angers me—striking—and after all, I'm not as old as all that." The remark about age had stung her as usual. Carmichael was deeply conscious of her age. Forty seemed so old, she thought as she picked up her fork. I've got to get the post of Nursing Officer, she decided as she bit into the kidney. There she was, stuck there on the orthopaedic ward. Still, she'd only been there a short time and she did feel her efficiency was unquestioned.

"Oh, come on, Carmichael, I mean you can't compare yourself with a kid of twenty. They think differently, and some of them are married and have got H.P. and have got a mortgage and God knows what. You don't have the same problems."

"Pardon me, I've got a mortgage," said Carmichael coldly.

"Well, there's only you," chimed in Hill. "You're not like me. My husband's out of work and he's only got the dole and our kid's allowance. I know he stops at home and does the housework, but it's not ideal, is it? He's not happy. If I could take more money home I'd be damn glad of it."

"Yes indeed, but what would you do without your job, if all this clamouring for money was to make the health service too expensive?" asked Carmichael.

Another Sister, older than Hill, Sister of the men's medical, a rather charming grey-haired woman, chimed in:

"Oh, don't give us that, please, Sister Carmichael. They've got the money when they want to make war with anybody. Don't talk to me about expense."

Carmichael did not speak again. The conversation was not going the way she liked. She didn't know quite what her views were about peace and war, but on the business of striking they were rigid.

As they came out of the nurses' dining-room the very porter they had been talking about went by them wheeling a trolley piled with linen. He grumbled as he passed them.

"I shouldn't be doing this—head porter—just because Jim's

off sick. He would be, wouldn't he. You'll all be grumbling if your linen is late, and there's nothing I can do about it. I'm two porters short."

"Well, there're plenty of unemployed to take those jobs, I should have thought." Carmichael's voice came from the back of the group, and Sampson looked up quickly. When he saw who had spoken, his face reddened.

"If the salaries were decent there'd be more of them. It's hardly worth them coming into bloody hospitals. They're better off on the dole if they've got kids. You should damn well know that."

"Oh, come now, that's not true, and please don't swear when you speak to me," said Carmichael and went on ahead of the other Sisters into the rest-room to have her coffee. They followed her.

"You'll get your linen later than ever today," said Hill, winking at the others.

"Yes, that's exactly the kind of thing that man would do, take it out on the patients," said Carmichael. The others could see that she was getting really enraged and her usually sallow neck was flushing up, so they went and helped themselves to coffee, took it over to a small table, and sat down.

The television was switched on to catch the last of Pebble Mill, and talk about strikes, industrial action, salaries, and Jack Sampson was for the moment dropped, but Carmichael knew only too well that it would start again the moment she was out of the room. She loathed this kind of talk. Nursing was a profession, a profession she was proud to be in, and she wouldn't do anything to injure it. They would—and that Jack Sampson. Something would have to be done about him. If she caught him again stirring up any of her young nurses she'd have something to say. If she couldn't stop him one way, no doubt she could another. If he wasn't careful she'd . . ."

Suddenly Carmichael felt very cold and shivered. One of the other Sisters noticed, because she said:

"It's not very warm in here, is it? They've probably turned the bloody heat off—Oh, sorry." She obviously remembered the remark Carmichael had made to Sampson about swearing. Carmichael was easily outraged. This time, however, she didn't seem to be, and she smiled her downward smile.

"No, a grey goose going over my grave, I suppose." For a moment the coldness lasted as if she was sitting in a draught. She got up and, although her coffee was only half-finished, left the room. The head porter's face seemed to dance in front of her, menacing all she stood for: integrity, loyalty to her patients . . . She was part of a great profession which he could ruin. She had seen demonstrations on television. Nurses, their hair and uniforms disarranged, shouting and screaming, and it was always more money they were after. Very often a man like Jack Sampson was leading them. Carmichael continued on her way to her wards. The picture she had conjured up was too horrible and she did her best to dismiss it from her mind, but it was difficult and Jack Sampson's sneering face and the demonstrating nurses continued to haunt her memory, making her feel almost physically sick, making her head ache. She wanted to get back to her ward as quickly as possible.

CHAPTER 5

Some days later Carmichael had another brush with Jack Sampson. The lifts at Greyfriars were a little temperamental, apt to stick sometimes six inches below a floor or perhaps six inches above, occasionally even as much as a foot. Carmichael had pointed this out to her Nursing Officer several times and, indeed, had grumbled about it to almost anyone who would listen, as had some of the other Sisters.

It could be troublesome, particularly when bringing a patient down from the theatre on a trolley. Several times the electricians had been called in to try and put the fault right, but with the talk of a new lift system being installed soon not much attention had been given to it.

On this day, after lunch, as Carmichael came up in the lift, it stuck about a foot below her floor. Carmichael found she could open the doors, and she stepped up out of the lift with some effort and with a great deal of annoyance showing on her face. Coming up the stairs was Geoff Miles, one of Carmichael's staff, a male nurse, a pleasant man about thirty. He gave Carmichael little or no trouble on the ward; indeed, they got on particularly well. Miles was quiet, went about his business with a minimum of fuss, and reported to Carmichael exactly what he had done or any unusual signs or symptoms among the patients.

"Having trouble?" he asked. Carmichael turned and was about to shut the doors when he came forward. "Oh," he went on, "it hasn't come right up. It's always doing this. They don't seem able to put it right, do they?"

Carmichael shook her head and looked inside the lift doors. "It's a great nuisance and it could cause trouble in an emergency, if they were taking a patient to or from the theatre. It's usually not quite as bad as this, though."

Miles nodded and, going in front of her with an "Excuse me, Sister," stepped down into the lift and proceeded to press the buttons rapidly, one by one.

"This sometimes does it—makes it jump up. I don't know why. There must be something wrong with the circuit behind this panel. I used to be a bit of an electrician before I started nursing."

Carmichael said, "Oh," rather disinterestedly and noticed that as he touched one of the buttons the lift did come creakily into position.

"Surely a lift shouldn't move when the doors are open?" Carmichael said.

Miles shook his head. "No, they shouldn't, that's just it, there's something wrong with the circuit."

He was standing there, his hand on the button in the lift, when Porter Sampson came to the top of the stairs. He'd been running up fairly briskly and was on his way to the theatre.

"Oh, it's you holding up the damn lift, is it? What do you think you're doing?"

"Sister came up and the lift didn't come to the floor properly. It was almost a foot down. It's really not good enough, you know. I've just been trying to . . . Well, there's something wrong with the wiring behind this panel, I think. You see, if you—"

Jack Sampson cut him off brusquely: "What's it to do with you? You're not an electrician, are you? Meddling in other people's jobs—that's something I just won't have. As shop steward, I have to see to it that the job's done by the person who's supposed to do it and not by any old Tom, Dick, or Harry who thinks he can put a finger in. How would you like it if I came and tried to put some of your catheters up, eh?"

The porter had completely ignored Carmichael, and her face crimsoned. "Don't speak like that to my Staff Nurse, please. He's not doing anything wrong. If the electricians were up to standard they would maintain the lifts properly. A patient could sue the hospital if any harm came to them because the lift was out of order."

"Oh, they could, could they? And you're a lawyer, are you? What a lot of you meddle in other people's business, talking about things you know nothing about. You know perfectly well they're going to put a new lift in and this old lift is going to be taken out."

"I'm well aware of that," said Carmichael, "but that doesn't alter the fact that at the moment they're still carrying patients up and down." She went on: "The lifts should be in proper working order or someone should be warned about them."

"Oh, perhaps you'd better go and do the warning then. You'll be able to see the head electrician and tell him what to do, and take 'this' with you." He cast a contemptuous glance towards Miles.

"Don't call me 'this,' " said Miles, moving aggressively towards him.

Carmichael put up her hand authoritatively. "That will do. Go into the ward, please, Staff Nurse Miles. Don't bandy words with the porter."

Miles looked at Carmichael, then back at Sampson, then, apparently deciding she was probably right, he marched towards the swing-doors leading to the ward, angrily pushing them open. They swung to behind him.

"Oh, you do what she says, do you? That's what I like to see, a man ordered about by a woman. Silly bugger," Sampson called after him.

Carmichael really lost her temper then. "Don't dare use language like that on this floor! If other people allow you to, then let them, but here you will behave properly. I shall report you to the hospital secretary and you might as well know it. I shall do it at nine tomorrow morning, so if he sends for you, you'll know what it's about."

"Oh yeah, I will. I shall report you too, so don't you forget it, meddling with the electrical apparatus. You know what they'll say about that. You know what it's like when it happens in the theatre. There have been several people reprimanded for trying to mend electrical things."

"And why?" queried Carmichael. "For the very same reason—the inefficiency of the electricians—because they go off at five and because they put such an addition on their wages if they're called back for overtime. Don't think I don't know. I wouldn't put it beyond them to leave things undone so that they have to come back. I know about these things, so don't think I'm not up to every trick in hospital," she said.

Jack Sampson could hardly speak he was so furious. "So that's what you think, is it, that's why you're so against the unions? I know you. Just as I said the other day, you'll let everyone else do everything, strike, demonstrate, or anything else and you wouldn't join in, but you'd take what came along in the way of rises, longer holidays, shorter hours, anything. You don't want to soil your hands with us, though, do you?" He turned on his heel and clattered down the stairs.

Carmichael went up to the lift doors and closed them carefully. She was trembling with rage and, because of this, refrained from banging the doors. The porters all lacked respect. That arrogant man! She intended to carry out her threat to report him to the hospital secretary, though perhaps it would do no good. Perhaps this beastly man had influence with the hospital's administrators. Nevertheless, this thought did not deter Carmichael's determination to report the whole disgraceful affair to the secretary in the morning.

Next morning it was not nine but nearly half past ten before Carmichael managed to get away from the ward and see Mr. Wills, the hospital secretary. She knocked loudly.

"Come." Carmichael pushed open the office door and walked in and she could see as she entered that Wills was not particularly pleased to see her. He was a great one for things going through the proper channels. A Sister coming in to see him direct was not correct and Carmichael was aware of it. She should have reported Sampson and the lift to her Nursing Officer and she in her turn would report it to her senior officer. However, Carmichael had already spoken to Miss O'Donoghue about the man's rudeness and it had got no further. This time she was determined to handle the matter herself.

She straightened her back as she crossed to the secretary's desk. He did not rise, neither did he offer her a chair, but Carmichael sat down anyway. This, too, obviously did not please him.

"Yes, Sister, what can I do for you?"

"I know this is not quite the procedure as you like it, Mr. Wills," said Carmichael, "but I've tried to report it to the right person and it seems to have had no effect. It's about Sampson, the head porter. I really can't have him speaking to me or my Staff Nurse in the manner in which he did yesterday. He was insolent."

"Excuse me, Sister, if I interrupt," he said pompously, "but does this concern the little brush you had about the lift?" Obviously he already knew all about it. Sampson must have been here before her this morning. As head porter he had every right to go to the hospital secretary.

"Yes, it does. He was—"

"Sister, before you go any further I would like to say this. You know, both you and your Staff Nurse, from what I understand from Sampson, were totally in the wrong. It is not the policy of this hospital to allow nursing staff to attempt to 'mend' or tamper in any way with electrical equipment. After all, that is why we keep electricians, and you know how strict the rules are. Even Sampson himself would not have touched that lift, and by the sound of it, from what I hear from him, it was a dangerous procedure anyway that your Staff Nurse was engaged in."

Carmichael broke in harshly: "Well, of course, Mr. Wills, if you're going to listen to a porter's story first and then not let me tell you mine at all—"

"Sister Carmichael, I would listen to your story if it were my job to do so. I am sure you know quite well you should have gone to your Nursing Officer."

"I have been to my Nursing Officer and nothing whatever has been done. The lift has been troublesome for some time, you must know that. If my report has gone through the proper channels then you must know that, and also you must know that nothing effective has been done."

"I do, Sister Carmichael. I am well aware that the lift is not as efficient as it should be. You must also be aware that we are taking out the whole system and putting in a new lift. This will entail a great deal of organization on the part of the administrative staff and collaboration between both the medical and the nursing staff. This is how things are done. The theatres will have to be closed; operations will cease while the lift is being put in. You must know that it is a big undertaking and we want to keep the present lift going as long and as near to the time of putting in the new one as possible. Now, perhaps that explanation will satisfy you."

"No, it will not," said Carmichael. "I came here not to complain about the lift only, but to complain about the head porter's behaviour, his way of speaking to me—and his language both to me and to Staff Nurse Miles."

"It sounds to me, Sister, that he had ample reason. After all, your Staff Nurse was tampering with the lift, trying to bring it up to the floor level with the doors open—"

"—and succeeding," said Carmichael. Her temper was rising and she felt a flush coming up her neck and both her cheeks, and a pulse was beating rapidly on her temple.

"He might well have succeeded, but he should not have been doing anything to the lift at all."

"I—" Carmichael attempted to speak but Mr. Wills cut her off.

"Sister Carmichael, I'm sorry, but I can't listen to any more of this. As I say, judging by what I hear, the porter was entirely right. You and your Staff Nurse were both wrong. If he was rude to you and used words that perhaps you found unpleasant, I am sorry, I apologize for him."

"Thank you very much, Mr. Wills. I suppose that it is really a trade union matter."

Wills looked up quickly. "It could be, indeed it could. It is very dangerous for anyone other than electrician to tamper with electrical equipment. You, Sister, would not want an electrician trying to nurse your patients. I'm afraid that is all I have to say on the matter." He rose to his feet and Carmichael had to rise too. She felt bitter but comforted herself as she stood there with the thought that there must be other ways to cope with this obnoxious little man.

"If you want to report this to your nursing administrators, please do," said Mr. Wills, "but I must warn you that I think they would say the same as I have. Now, Sister, that is all."

Carmichael turned on her heel and walked across the room and opened the office door. She looked back at him.

"It seems to me that you're afraid of Sampson. He seems to do as he likes, goes round trying to get people to join his union, talking to my nurses and trying to persuade them."

"And what is wrong with that?" asked Wills, looking at her with direct antagonism.

Carmichael was silent. She couldn't fight the system, she thought, but again there must be other ways. She walked out of the office, closing the door none too softly behind her.

As she left, Carmichael came face to face with Jack Sampson. The smile on his face indicated that he knew pretty well the reception she had had in the secretary's office.

"You and Mr. Wills have a cosy little chat, then, Sister?"

Carmichael went to pass him and tried to ignore his remarks, but he persisted, turning his trolley at an angle which blocked her way forward.

"Will you please move that trolley, Sampson."

"Mr. Sampson to you, Sister," the porter replied, not attempting to move the obstruction. Carmichael put her hand out and pushed the trolley violently to one side.

"Temper, temper, Sister," he said, as a pile of sheets lurched sideways and he just managed to save them from falling.

"You haven't heard the last of this." Carmichael was almost incapable of speech. This on top of the secretary's rebuff was too much. She was closer to tears of sheer rage than she felt she had ever been before.

"Neither have you, if you play about with that lift again, or your pansy Staff Nurse." Sampson jerked the trolley sideways and wheeled it rapidly down the corridor.

Carmichael made for the stairs. She arrived at her ward and went into her office. Her head ached, throbbing violently, and it continued to do so all day.

"It looks like an awful storm coming up, Sister," said Junior Nurse Chapman. "You've got a car, though, haven't you? I'd like to ring up my boy-friend. I'm frightened of thunder and lightning. I'm not going home in it on my own. I'll get him to come and fetch me."

Carmichael looked at her. She was preoccupied still. Sampson's remarks and his behaviour, the scene in Wills's office would not leave her. She felt humiliated. She had not been able to eat lunch and had not even gone to the dining-room for tea. She tried to drag herself away from her preoccupation and looked out of the window. Yes, the sky was black, almost copper-coloured.

"It certainly looks horrible," she said. Sheet lightning streaked across the sky, followed by a low distant rumble of thunder.

The little nurse shivered. "Oh, let me go to the phone, Sister. May I make a personal call? Up here on the ward phone, I mean, and get my boy-friend to call for me when I'm off in ten minutes?"

Carmichael nodded. She didn't like thunderstorms much herself, but she was not afraid of them. It was safe in a car, she had always heard, because of the rubber tyres.

"Yes, Nurse, all right, telephone him," she said benignly, much to the nurse's surprise. She knew Sister Carmichael didn't usually allow personal calls from the ward. Normally you had to ask permission to leave the ward and went all the way down the stairs to the public phone box, but for once she was being nice. Nurse Chapman went to ring up the boy-friend.

Why do they all have boy-friends, thought Carmichael, and suddenly she was more conscious of her aching head and filled with a terrible dreariness. She rebuked herself sharply. Now pull yourself together, all that's over. She'd got a lovely cottage, two beautiful cats, and a new car. For goodness' sake, what more do you want? Nothing, she told herself, as she went into the ward and called the Staff Nurse to give the report before she went home.

She was off at six. The day had not been pleasant for her, what with one thing and another. This afternoon had been better than the morning, but her head had ached. Maybe it was the coming storm as well as Sampson. She meant to go home and cook herself a meal—it would be a change from the nurses' dining-room. The food wasn't bad, but it was nice to have a home-cooked meal. She knew waiting at home was a small fillet steak that she had taken out of the freezer and put into the refrigerator before she had left that morning, and there would be Tibbles and Torty waiting to greet her. Her depression retreated a little but did not go away completely.

As she drove home she thought ruefully that she so seldom used the lift. On leaving the Sisters' rest-room she had met Mr. Parsons from the consultants' dining-room. He'd stopped her to ask after one or two of his patients in order, Carmichael suspected, to save himself having to come up to the ward. This had delayed her, so on this occasion she had broken her self-imposed rule and taken the lift. With what a result, she thought bitterly, with what a result!

CHAPTER 6

As Carmichael drove home the storm worsened. The lightning was flashing and the thunder crashing almost overhead, whereas when the nurse on Carmichael's ward started to ring her boy-friend the thunder had been a distant rumble. Carmichael smiled at the thought of her nurse. Stupid girl, what use did she think a boy-friend would be in a storm?

She drove along the road slowly because the rain was pouring down and the autumn evening was darker than usual. The rain made driving difficult. As she got nearer home and took the right-hand fork down a narrowish lane towards the cottage she suddenly noticed a car, stationary on the side of the road, its bonnet up and a man bending, peering into the engine. It was a large, old car and Carmichael thought she recognized it. As she approached, the man stepped into the middle of the road looking directly at her and she realized she'd often seen his car parked outside the hospital. It was Jack Sampson. She drew up, her bonnet almost touching him. It was only then that he appeared to realize who she was.

"Oh, it's Sister Carmichael. Can't expect any help from you, I suppose," he shouted sarcastically, making himself heard above the rain.

Carmichael wound her window down and put her head out of the window. "I'm always ready to help anyone who needs help, Mr. Sampson," she said coldly.

"Well . . . if you could get in the car and start her up when I tell you. I can't do both, you see."

Carmichael wound up her window and then got out of her car.

Sampson went on: "See, it's not in gear."

She got into the front seat of Sampson's old banger. The car smelled of beer and she noticed behind the passenger seat one or two empty cans. She wrinkled her nose in distaste. She could see nothing—the bonnet obscured the view through the windscreen.

Suddenly she heard Jack Sampson call, "Now, turn her on."

Carmichael twisted the key in the ignition. The batteries seemed to be working, as far as she could tell. There was not the slow, deadly wail they made when they were flat or about to fail. The engine, however, did not pick up. Carmichael leaned out of the window and Sampson peered round the bonnet at her.

"Turned it off, have you?"

Carmichael called back, "Yes."

They were both speaking loudly. The rain now was beating on the roof of the big car. In the murky light Carmichael could see it pouring down Sampson's face, and it gave her some satisfaction. "Serve him right," she said under her breath and settled back in the seat. She had a little time to spare, there was no rush. She rather liked to see his discomfort.

On Sampson's instructions she tried again, but the engine would not start in spite of his fiddling about under the bonnet.

He called again, "Right, have another go."

Carmichael turned on the ignition once more, pressed the starter again, and Sampson's face, slightly more hopeful, peered round the bonnet.

"Go on, go on," he said. "I think she's picking up. Just touch the accelerator." His words were drowned as suddenly the engine roared into life. "Thank God for that, the buggering thing," he yelled and came round to the side of the car.

As he did so Carmichael had an idea. It flashed across her mind like a picture in a second. She knew what she was going to do. She smiled, not the same smile that had twisted her lips when she thought of her little nurse and the boy-friend, but a downward, strange smile. Now she would pay him out for trying to seduce the nurses into striking.

Carmichael looked him full in the face and said, "Mr. Sampson, your bonnet's not properly closed."

He turned. "Oh hell, it never closes properly. You have to bang it. Hang on." He went to the front of the car and put the flat of his hand on the bonnet and pushed. The bonnet closed, then sprang open again. He gave it another push with the heel of his hand. As he did this Carmichael took off the brake. The engine was still running. She pushed the lever into first gear and drove it forward. There was a cry as Jack Sampson toppled backwards. Carmichael turned the steering-wheel a little and edged the car slightly more forward. There was a bump, a crunch—then silence. She wanted to be sure. She straightened up the wheels with difficulty, backed, then drove forward again. There was another bump and again complete silence broken by a crash of thunder overhead. The rain beat on mercilessly.

As she removed her foot from the clutch the engine stalled. She switched off the ignition and put the gear into neutral, got out of the car, leaving the door open, and went round to the front. There was no movement. Jack Sampson lay partially under the car. One of the wheels had gone across his chest, blood was oozing out from the front of his shirt, quite a lot of blood, and the side of his chest had a squashed look. There was also blood trickling from his mouth. Carmichael stooped and put a practised finger on the carotid artery. His head was bent backwards at an uncomfortable angle that reminded her of Emily at the foot of the stairs a long time ago. Did she feel a pulse, a slight flicker? She couldn't be quite sure. She pressed her finger again with distaste on the throat. No. A flash of lightning lit the face, which looked wide-eyed, surprised. Carmichael did not think it necessary to investigate further. She looked round the scene with an expert eye, then, noting that the bonnet was not properly closed, she put her fingers underneath the rim and pushed. It rose in the air immediately on a spring. She stepped back, the water running off the skirt of her mackintosh. The driver's door of the car was open, the bonnet up and the prone body underneath. It was a wonderful picture of an accident.

She looked carefully at the surface of the road. No, no car track would show that she had been there. And what if it did? The water was gushing down both sides of the road. She took one more look at Sampson, then got into her car, started the engine, and drove off unhurriedly towards her cottage.

She was a little worried about the cats. She hoped they'd had the sense to come in out of the rain. They usually did. Sometimes she bolted the cat-door and kept them in when it was pouring, but this morning when she had set off for the hospital the sun had been shining. Would the storm have frightened them? She dismissed the thought of the dead man and drove on, her windscreen wipers working at top speed.

When she arrived home it was still just light enough to see the cottage and the trees surrounding it. In fact, it seemed a little lighter and the rain was easing but still unpleasant. The thunder rumbled, farther away now, and the sheet lightning lit up the sky. She put the car in the garage and went in the front door. She called the cats. On a fine summer evening they would be outside and she would hear the bang of the cat-flap as they came through it, but today only Torty was in and she came up to her immediately, tail erect and fluffy, her round orange eyes looking up at her with what Carmichael took to be great affection.

"Tibbles," she called, but there was no sign of the other cat.

In the kitchen she unlocked and opened the back door and went out, making the cat-flap swing as she did so. The apple trees were drenched and dripping. She stood calling and then heard a miaowing somewhere in the direction of the trees. She continued calling and then saw, to her dismay, as a bright flash of lightning lit up the garden, Tibbles high on one of the apple tree branches. Whether she was so terrified of the thunder that she was paralysed with fright and unable to move, Carmichael didn't know. Both cats climbed the trees regularly. Poor Tibbles, she was soaked, and at the sight of Carmichael her miaowing grew louder.

Carmichael ran to the bottom of the garden, flung open the shed door, and got a pair of steps the gardener sometimes used to clean the upper windows of the cottage. He came once a week now, everything was well organized, and Carmichael rarely had to cope with an emergency, but this . . . She carried the steps back to the tree, tried to make them firm in the wet grass, then, holding on to the trunk and the steps, climbed upwards.

Tibbles saw her coming and miaowed even louder. Carmichael had to stand precariously on the top step, steadying herself against the tree with the other hand. Then she just managed to reach the cat. It clung to the branch and she almost had to tear the claws away. Dripping and wet, it crouched in Carmichael's arm while she made her way carefully down the steps.

She went into the house, crooning to the cat. She put Tibbles down, got a large bath towel, and rubbed its body and tail. Soon the frightened creature began to purr, to Carmichael's satisfaction.

She left it for a moment, struck a match, and lit the paper under the wood and coal in the grate. It was not really cold enough for a fire, but this evening was exceptional. The rain outside, the unusual darkness, and the terrified animal necessitated something comforting.

Carmichael went on drying the cat, Torty looking on apprehensively. At last she considered her dry enough, went through to the kitchen, closed the back door, and slid the little bolt in the cat-door. They could stay in now. Both cats were miaowing round her feet, Tibbles's fear apparently forgotten. Carmichael looked down at them consumed with affection.

Just like before, Tibbles, she thought, I remember when you were wet once before, when you ran out into the rain with me from that terrible house. She dismissed the thought. She didn't want to think about that. It was a long while ago.

Carmichael went to the cupboard and took out a large tin of cat food, opened it, and tipped half of the contents onto one plate and the other half on the other. She put the plates down on a cat mat, and both animals set to vigorously, their bodies going fatter as they ate, their tails sticking out behind them, straight on the kitchen floor.

She skirted them and went round to the refrigerator, got out the small fillet steak, took the grill from the electric stove, placed it on the working surface, then, taking butter from the fridge, she cut a piece off and smoothed it over the steak. As she did so her eyes strayed for a moment to the plate on which the steak had rested. Exactly under it, where the meat had been, was a small ring of blood. For the first time since entering the cottage Carmichael thought of Jack Sampson lying there in the rain, blood on the tufted grass. It was not a pretty picture and she dismissed it. Holding the plate under the hot tap, she washed away the red blood till it became just a pink stain, then she took a mop from a jam jar at the side of the sink and rubbed the mop head vigorously on the plate till the last remnant of blood disappeared.

She turned on the electric ring under the vegetables which she had prepared before she went out in the morning. Then, just as carefully, she turned on the grill low.

In the sitting-room the fire was burning up now and looked cheerful against the dreary evening. Carmichael smiled to herself, another smile, this one of complete contentment. She drew the curtains on the lightning and dripping garden, frowned a little as she saw that the heavy rain had beaten the asters down, then she turned away, bent down, and switched on the television. She was just in time for "Brookside."

CHAPTER 7

Helen Sampson opened the oven door and looked inside at her husband's supper. Jack was late again. Of course he'd tell her that he'd had an extra job to do at the hospital but he'd come in reeking of beer. Helen knew her husband only too well. She listened to the storm outside. She was not nervous about either thunder or lightning but she was thinking of her friend Doris Pilcher coming to fetch her to go to bingo. Doris wasn't too keen on storms, and she hoped it wouldn't put her off. As if in answer to her thoughts a bang came on the front door. Helen went through and opened it. Doris stood outside.

"For God's sake, let me in. I think I'm damn good coming in all this. Something awful, isn't it?" she said.

Helen opened the door wider. "Not very good, I agree, but it'll be all right in the Scala, ducks." She hurried back into the kitchen where she had left the oven door open.

"Jack home yet?" queried Doris.

"No. I'm not bothered. I told him I was going to bingo so he can just put up with it. I've put his supper in the oven and it's drying up already, but that's his funeral." She banged the oven door shut and walked into the hall, picked up a mackintosh, put it on, then tied a scarf over her head.

"Come on, let's go. I feel lucky tonight," she said.

Her friend laughed. "I've heard you say that before and come away with nothing."

"Well, it's somewhere to go, for God's sake. Can't stick in this place all the time. That's what Jack would like. As long as I'm sitting by the telly and knitting, he's happy—that is, when he condescends to come home. Well, I'll be out tonight." She pulled the door closed behind her and pushed it to see if the latch had caught. "Come on, let's get cracking."

The two women hurried down the short garden path and got into the red car. Doris Pilcher started the engine, ducked a little as another flash of lightning lit the sky and the thunder rumbled quickly after it.

"That means it's close, that does. That means it's coming back," she said, backing out into the lane. "When the thunder comes straight after the lightning, they say if you count in between the flash and the rumble then you know how far away it is, in miles, see?"

"That's not far away then, is it?" said Helen. "But you're all right in a car, you know. It's the rubber tyres, see?" Helen went on reassuringly.

"Well, I must say I've never heard of a car being struck, but it could strike your house, you know. You don't seem to care."

"No, that would cook his dinner nicely, wouldn't it?" Helen Sampson cackled and Doris joined her.

They drove along in silence for a moment or two, Helen opening her bag and taking out a packet of cigarettes, lighting one for Doris and one for herself. The windscreen wipers threw the water to each side. Doris drove leaning forward slightly as she looked through the rain. There was still some light left but the evening aided by the low rainstorm clouds was much darker than it would normally have been at that time.

"Why don't you put your lights on? It's not lighting-up time yet but it might help," said Helen, leaning forward as well, to peer through the downpour.

"Don't want to. Battery's low. Won't get us home then."

"Oh, God! I hope it will be all right, for goodness' sake," said Helen.

"Oh, it'll be all right, don't worry, but I don't want to risk it. I can see all right." Doris drove on and as they rounded a corner they saw in front of them a car, its door open and its bonnet up.

Helen let out a shriek of laughter. "Look, it's Jack's car, the bugger's broken down. He's had to go off somewhere to get help, I expect. He could have walked home, really. Wonder he didn't. Just like him to leave the whole thing. Perhaps he's got a mate with him, though. I expect they've gone to the pub."

"Shall I stop?" asked Doris, looking into the empty car as they drove by.

"No, what's the use. It'll only make us late getting to bingo and he's probably happy in the pub anyway. Gone there for help and stayed there for drinks. Silly bastard—leaving the door open—just like him. No, leave him to it. Serve him right."

"O.K., then. He can't be far away or he wouldn't have left the door open and the bonnet up like that in this rain. The engine will be soaked, and that won't help."

The two women drove on, chuckling to themselves. They arrived at the Scala and parked the car. The car park was unusually empty, probably because of the storm. They got out and Doris clattered on her high heels, followed by Helen, who was limping slightly.

"Wait for me, for goodness' sake, you know what my knee's like. And what about the car? Shouldn't you have locked it?" asked Helen breathlessly. Once inside she took off her headscarf and shook it to get the water off.

"No, nothing in it to steal, and anyway who'd want that car? When we come out it will probably be raining and if there's anything I hate it's having to unlock a car in the pouring rain." Doris threw the keys into her handbag, took off her rain hat and shook the glistening drops onto the floor. They went towards the office to pay.

"Good luck, ladies," said the man issuing them their bingo cards.

"Thanks," said Helen, and the two women moved away from the little office from where the cards were sold.

"I could fancy him," said Helen.

"Oh, get away, he's as old as God's dog," said her friend.

"I don't care," said Helen. "He's got those distinguished

grey bits of hair by the side of his head. I rather go for that. I like him. Probably got some grey hairs other places too."

"Ooh, you are awful," said Doris, and the swing-doors into the big hall closed behind them.

At eleven o'clock the bingo hall disgorged its chattering clients, Doris and Helen among them. Both their faces were lighted up with acquisitive delight. Doris had won four hundred pounds in the grand card bingo game, and they always shared their winnings. Two hundred pounds each—what a windfall! Doris giggled excitedly as they both got into the car and as she fell back into the driver's seat, clutching her handbag on her lap, she turned to Helen and their eyes met and they again became convulsed with laughter.

"You going to tell him? Jack, I mean?" asked Doris, and Helen shook her head vehemently.

"Not on your nelly. He'll think he should have half of it. No. I say let's go and have a drink."

"Why not?" answered Doris.

"Don't expect he's home yet," went on Helen. "If he is, he'll have something to say about the state of his dinner for sure, unless some floozie has cooked one for him. Can't see what they see in him, but they do see something. Wonder if he got the car started?"

Doris opened her handbag, peeped in, then snapped the bag shut.

"Good heavens, I hope we're not mugged," she giggled.

"Well, if we are I hope it's somebody good-looking."

Neither of the women could stop laughing, though they'd had nothing to drink but coffee in the bingo hall. They both felt slightly intoxicated with their win. Doris drove out of the car park and onto the road.

"Let's go and have a quick one—in the Blue Boar—bit of a laugh, eh? I don't often go into a pub by myself. It'll be rather nice, just the two of us, no blooming men looking down their noses if you order a short."

"Well, I suppose I shouldn't. He'll smell it on my breath . . ."

"So what? He's in the pub often enough. I wouldn't think he could smell anything on anybody else's breath but his own," Doris said, and Helen nodded.

"All right, then, we'll go and have just one," she said.

Doris drove the car expertly into one of the few remaining car spaces outside the Blue Boar. They went into the bar and Doris ordered two whiskies. Helen, of course, had to buy one back and she made these doubles, reasoning to herself that they were pretty near home and, anyway, Doris was used to drink.

They finished their second whisky with enjoyment, making plans about what they were going to do with the money, how they'd hide it from their husbands. They'd stash it away somewhere, spend it bit by bit on something they wanted, so that their men folk wouldn't suspect. The fact that it was a secret made it even more exciting.

When they got outside the Blue Boar the storm had started again. During their time in the hall it had ceased and the rumbling of thunder had died away, but now it was back. A sharp, cold wind blew and Helen shivered.

"Come on, let's get cracking. It's going to rain again." She had hardly said it before big drops started to patter onto the already wet forecourt of the pub. They dashed to the car and got inside, breathless but still laughing. A heavy rumble of thunder, then a flash of lightning and more thunder made both women squeal. Helen banged the door on her side and belted up and Doris, already in the car, started up the engine.

They drove out to the road, Doris driving carefully. The windscreen wipers again splashed the water to and fro.

"Put your lights on now, for God's sake," Helen said, and Doris stopped the car with a jerk, throwing Helen forward against the seat-belt.

"Sorry, damn it, I forgot." Doris Pilcher switched the lights on and a beam cut through the falling rain. Another flash of lightning made Helen jump, then a crackle of thunder.

"That's right overhead, it bloody well would be," said Doris. "Hope this rain doesn't stop the car. It does sometimes. It's a bit dodgy, this car."

"Now you tell me," she said, but there was not really much worry in her tone. The whisky had mellowed her.

They drove along out of the town and started down the road that led to the turning that would eventually land them at Helen's house.

"Hope to God the road's not flooded," said Doris as they approached the turning.

"Well, we've got to go that way. There's no other way. That's what comes of living in a damn hollow. I'm always saying we're off the beaten track—too much so for my liking," said Helen. She was trying to see herself in her compact held close to her face. She was putting powder on her nose.

"You doing that from memory?" asked Doris, and Helen, now putting on lipstick, nodded and said:

"Just about."

Suddenly Doris almost stopped the car. The headlights had lighted up Sampson's car in the near distance.

"Look at that," said Doris, "that bloody car's still there. That fathead of a husband of yours has gone off and got drunk, that's what he's done. Got fed up with the car, I expect. Look, the door's still open and the bonnet."

"He must be dotty," said Helen. "Stop the car and I'll get out and close the bonnet and the door at least. There's no need to have the thing soaked through—although it is by now."

Doris stopped the car and Helen scrambled out. She peered inside and slammed the door, then went forward to close the bonnet. From the car Doris, fumbling in her bag for a cigarette, watched her. She saw Helen put her hand up to the bonnet as she stood at the side of the car, as if she was about to slam it down. Then it appeared to Doris that she couldn't make it close from the side, for she moved a little more, into a better position in the front of the car. As she did so she appeared to stumble and looked down. Then Doris heard her scream, a long blood-curdling scream, closely followed by another crack of thunder above her head. Doris undid her seatbelt, scrambled out of the car, came round, crossed through the beam of her headlights, and looked down at what Helen had seen.

"My God!" she said.

CHAPTER 8

In Casualty that night, at about midnight, the two nurses on duty could still hear the thunder rumbling.

"Oh, it's hot in here. I've got such a headache, too." Staff Nurse Reynolds passed one hand across her forehead, her elbow resting on the desk. She'd been writing in the Casualty book, but now she leaned back tiredly and stretched.

"It's going to be one of those long nights. I wish something would come in. It would make the time go quicker." Her junior nurse came out of the big dressing-room.

"What?" she said. The Staff Nurse repeated her remark and looked at her junior more closely.

"What are you doing in there? You look flaked out. Have you been to bed today?"

Nurse Andrews nodded, then put her hand up and rubbed her eyes. "It must be the storm. I feel tired and, I don't know . . . Hot, isn't it?"

"You haven't been listening to a word I've said," said the Staff Nurse crossly. "I was saying I'd got a headache and asking what you were doing."

The junior nurse looked at her still rather vaguely. "Oh, I was just renewing the Elastoplast in there." She jerked her head backwards towards the dressing-room.

"Oh." Staff Nurse Reynolds relapsed back into her gloomy silence and resumed writing.

"I shall be glad when rest time comes and I can go off and get a meal. Maybe—I wish a casualty would be brought in, I really hope so," said Nurse Andrews, verifying the fact that she had not been listening to her Staff Nurse.

This exchange of conversation was typical of night duties,

Nurse Reynolds thought. The beginning of the night was always the worst, up to about two o'clock, then things got better somehow, as if you were running downhill instead of up. She anticipated going off duty at eight-thirty in the morning. Well, that was a long way off. Staff Reynolds didn't like night duty much, but they paid you more, and of course Andrews had to do it—she was still in training.

Just as Andrews was about to walk back into the dressing-room there was a sound of wheels on asphalt at the back of the hospital into the yard in which was situated the big storeroom, a small lodge for porters, the mortuary and, at the far end, a special small building where the badly soiled linen was sorted. Staff Reynolds raised her head from her book to listen.

"What's that? Someone coming in the back? Go and have a look."

Nurse Andrews turned, walked through the waiting-room, through the swing-doors, across the tiny tiled lobby, and opened the large back door, big enough to allow the passing of trolleys full of stores and, Nurse Andrews thought with a little shudder, deaders, on their way to the mortuary. She peered out into the night. The yard looked wet and sinister. An ambulance drew a little farther in, its rear doors coming nearer to the mortuary. Andrews thought automatically, B.I.D.— Brought in Dead. She knew the jargon now. When she first came to the hospital it had all been too complicated. She couldn't understand what the nurses meant when they said to each other "It's an R.T.A." or "a B.I.D." or "an O.D." Well, she had known what it meant when they said O.D.—who didn't?

She watched with interest tinged with apprehension as the ambulance men dropped down from the front, came round, opened the doors of the ambulance, drew out the steps. As they opened the doors light flooded onto the yard. Then one made his way to the side of the dirty linen sorting house where three metal trolleys stood under shelter out of the rain. He drew one forward and it made a clattering noise on the rough surface of the yard. Nurse Andrews called out, professionally, in an outraged voice:

"Not so much noise, please."

He grinned back at her. "Sorry, love," he said. "It won't wake the dead, though." He nodded towards the ambulance.

"They're not all dead in the hospital. What is it, then?" Andrews asked, she also indicating the ambulance.

"R.T.A. You'll be surprised when I tell you who it is," the ambulance man answered. His mate pulled out what was obviously a dead body, swathed in a red blanket, strapped onto a stretcher, round what Andrews assumed to be the legs and the chest. Again she shivered slightly. The rain, the humidity, the occasional flashes of lightning made it like a scene from a horror film.

"I'll be surprised, will I? Well, you'd better tell me who it is." She tried to sound flip. After all, nurses had to take this kind of thing. It happened every day. You'd got to learn to, well, show you were used to it.

"It's your head porter, Jack Sampson, that's who it is. Hallo, Bob." This last was said to a night porter who had come out, bringing some keys in his hand to open up the mortuary. He flung the doors back and the ambulance men wheeled their burden inside. The doors shut noisily behind them.

Jack Sampson! Well, that was something to tell her Staff Nurse. Nurse Andrews knew him fairly well. He was never on nights; he was shop steward of some union. She closed the big door. There was nothing more to see in that part of the hospital, only the gaping, lighted doors of the ambulance and the shut doors of the mortuary. The ambulance would drive off, leaving poor Jack Sampson behind. She tried to remember more about him besides what he looked like. She couldn't. Was he married, did he have any children, how old was he? Quite old, Nurse Andrews thought.

She tried to amass the details in her mind from memory as she went through the waiting-room and into Casualty to break the news.

Staff Nurse Reynolds was no longer sitting at her desk. While her junior nurse had been outside, a man had come into Casualty and Staff Nurse was attending to him in the dressing-room. For a moment the news would have to wait. Andrews went through to see what Staff Nurse Reynolds was doing.

"Well, how did you get it in there, for goodness' sake?" She was asking.

"I was trying to poke some wax out of my ear. It itched. I was trying to scratch it and the match broke." The man turned his ear again toward the Staff Nurse, who was standing poised with a pair of forceps.

"Does it hurt you?" she asked, and the man shook his head.

Nurse Andrews drew nearer, her curiosity about what the man had got in his ear overcoming for the moment her eagerness to impart the terrible news.

"Let this be a lesson to you, Nurse Andrews. This patient was scratching his ear with a matchstick and it broke. Sit down, please"—this to the patient, who sat down obediently—and the Staff Nurse switched on the light above the couch, angling it towards the man's ear. The match could be seen clearly and with the pair of forceps Reynolds carefully removed it. There was no blood on the end of it and the man did not even wince.

"Oh, thanks. I was a bit worried. I thought I'd better not go to bed with it in. I mean, when I went to sleep it might have rammed it in further. Thanks."

"You're welcome, but you'd better go and see your doctor in the morning."

The man got up and made for the door. His breath smelled of beer, but he didn't appear to be drunk.

"Aren't you going to enter him in the book?" asked Nurse Andrews.

Reynolds still stood beside the couch examining the match in the forceps in her hand, then she dropped both into the kidney dish she had brought with her. She shook her head.

"Oh no, for goodness' sake. There was no need to get our doctor out of bed."

"I thought we weren't allowed to treat anything ourselves, not without calling a doctor," said Nurse Andrews.

"We're not, but if you'd called out the Casualty officer for that—I expect the poor devil has only just gone to bed anyway—he wouldn't be best pleased, I can tell you. Don't say anything about it. Least said, soonest mended. Right?"

"Right, Staff. I've got something to tell you—about who it was they brought into the mortuary." Andrews paused and Staff Nurse Reynolds looked at her with some interest.

"Well, what? Don't keep me in suspense," she said half-sarcastically.

"Jack Sampson, our head porter, R.T.A.," she said. "Dead."

"Well, I'd hardly expect him to be alive if he's been taken to the mortuary. I hope the ambulance men haven't got that dim yet," answered the Staff Nurse, still with a sarcastic ring in her voice. She was not much affected by the death of the head porter, who seldom appeared on night duty, and she'd been on night duty long enough to have almost forgotten him, but she did go as far as to ask the decent questions.

"How did it happen? Wonder if his wife knows. He's married, isn't he? Car smashed up?"

"I didn't ask. They just said he was dead. That's all."

"Well, I suppose there'll be a collection for a wreath," said Staff Nurse Reynolds.

CHAPTER 9

At one a.m. just as Staff Nurse Reynolds was going to her meal, three people pushed their way straight through the waiting-room and into Casualty. The moment Reynolds saw them she felt they meant trouble.

The manner of two of them—there were two boys and a girl—was belligerent and threatening. The girl was half-supporting the boy in the middle who was clutching his right elbow, which was wrapped in a leather coat. The girl's heavily made-up eyes glared at Reynolds before she spoke, and her pouting lips with purple lipstick moved constantly as she chewed on the gum in her mouth. Matching rouge on the cheek-bones reaching almost to her ears made her look in the neon lights of Casualty like a heart case. Her hair, frizzed and plaited, was bright, bright yellow.

The boy on the other side was a skinhead. A bluish stubble of growth covered his scalp, and the aggressive look on his face was almost a copy of that on the girl's. The tight jeans and army camouflage jacket over a string vest did not match up well with the girl's more expensive punk clothes. She had a skin-tight top, stretched over breasts that were large for her slight frame, black knickerbockers, and ankle boots with high heels. They were like a picture from Top of the Pops, Reynolds thought. Then she saw the ashen face of the boy between them. This boy was wearing a yellow T-shirt, and across the chest, written in black letters, was "I hate the fuzz."

"What's he done to himself?" asked Reynolds, coming forward quickly.

"He's hurt his elbow. It's bashed, that's what it is, and it doesn't look too good," said the girl.

They stood there holding the boy between them as if reluctant to let him go, but Nurse Reynolds put her arm round the patient's waist, pushing aside the girl, who backed off reluctantly.

"Come with me," she said gently.

"Where does he have to go? We've got to go with 'im. Don't know what you get up to in these places." The boy spoke and Staff Reynolds did not think it was the time to argue.

"Right," she said, "I'll take him through. Come with me. Nurse Andrews, bring a Casualty card." They all went through into the big dressing-room and with difficulty the boy got up onto the couch to which Staff Nurse Reynolds led him, his dirty trainers making a mark on the white sheet.

"Take his shoes off, Nurse," said the Staff Nurse.

The girl and the boy were, by this time, standing back a little, watching.

"Let's see what you've done."

The injured boy had not spoken but lay with his head on the back rest that the nurse had raised for him. He put up a protesting hand, fingers stretched wide over the injured arm, as the nurse carefully unwound the coat.

"I must have a look, you know. Does it hurt very much?" Reynolds asked quietly.

"Does it hurt? That's a bloody silly question," said the girl. "You wait till you see it."

Staff Nurse Reynolds had seen it. She folded back the coat and found the injury to the elbow was considerable. The bone was showing, and the elbow joint looked as if it was dislocated. Nurse Andrews wheeled a trolley to the couch, then, on her senior's instructions, asked the boy and the girl to go out into the waiting-room.

The girl had gone pale under her rouge when she saw the arm, though obviously she was seeing it for the second time. She turned away and followed the junior nurse without question, and after a moment the boy followed too as the girl flung over her shoulder the remark:

"Better leave him, Doug, she knows what she's doing—I hope."

They went through into the waiting-room and Nurse Andrews followed them, carrying her pen and the Casualty card.

"What's his name, please?" she asked, standing in front of them as they sat down on the waiting-room chairs.

"Leo—Leo Kalinsky. He lives in School Lane, number six," answered Doug.

"Telephone number?" asked Nurse Andrews unwisely, and the boy guffawed and looked at the girl.

"Telephone number, silly cow, as if he'd have a telephone number. He lives in those flats, you know, high-rise, bloody awful."

Nurse Andrews said, "I'm sorry, I didn't think."

"You're paid to think," said the girl, crossing one knee over the other and showing the high spiky heel of her boot.

"How did it happen? It's a bad injury. How did he manage to hurt his arm like that?" asked Nurse Andrews rather timidly. They looked so threatening, both of them.

"Well, we were having a bit of an argument with two friends." He stopped and glanced sideways with narrowed eyes at the girl, whose face was expressionless. "We were having a bit of a rumble, see, and, well . . . we got the better of them, but they got in a car and drove it at us. We jumped, but Leo, he didn't jump far enough, he left his arm behind like and got it squashed between the wing of the car and the wall."

"What a terrible thing," said Nurse Andrews, for a moment jolted out of her professionalism. "Didn't you tell the police or anything?"

"Tell the fuzz? You must be joking. Of course we didn't. The others drove off. I don't suppose it even dented the wing. Might have, though, the way it dented his arm. Still, it was an old banger, anyway, no one would notice an extra dent, and you can't see the fuzz looking for our blood on the wing of a car."

Nurse Andrews looked bewildered but filled in on the Casualty card: "Elbow crushed between car and wall." It was the best she could do.

"Religion?" she asked, again timidly.

"Religion!" said the girl and went off into a peal of shrill laughter. "Well, let's see now, just a minute, he has a St. Christopher round his neck."

"No, he hasn't, they snatched it off. It was silver I think, but I don't think he's an R.C. Put down C. of E. That's what everybody puts, isn't it?"

Nurse Andrews nodded helplessly.

"Age?"

" 'E's seventeen, isn't 'e, Jane?" The girl nodded, leaning slightly sideways, trying to get something out of the pocket of her tight knickerbockers.

"I think so," she said.

"The name of his doctor?"

"Dunno," said the boy. "You'll 'ave to ask 'im. Dunno if 'e's even got one."

"What about his parents? We shall have to let them know."

"Much 'is dad'll care. You can try, if 'e's sober. 'Is mum ran off ages ago."

Nurse Andrews went through and put the card on the desk for Staff Nurse Reynolds to read later. She was giving the boy a shot of anti-tetanus as her junior came through.

"It was squashed between a car and a wall—his elbow, I mean," said Nurse Andrews, and Staff Reynolds nodded.

"So he's been saying. Stay with him," she said briefly. She went through to her desk and Andrews heard her ringing the night Casualty officer, Dr. Patel.

"I know, Doctor, but it's a badly injured elbow. Shall I ring X-ray? Well, normally I wouldn't do until you'd seen him, but it's a compound and the elbow is quite badly shattered. It'll take—Oh, all right."

Nurse Andrews, looking through from the dressing-room as she stood by the boy's couch, saw her senior sigh as she depressed the phone button to dial again. This time the person at the other end took some time to answer, but eventually Staff Nurse Reynolds spoke:

"Mrs. Haslemere? Yes—well, I know it's—But it's quite a nasty one, and Dr. Patel says to get you." The Staff Nurse put her hand over the mouthpiece and looked towards Nurse Andrews and raised her eyes to heaven, then turned back to the phone again. "All right . . . yes . . . no, I don't think so, the storm's gone over." She put the phone down and went back into the dressing-room.

"Mrs. Haslemere is on call for X-ray. She will be here soon. And Dr. Patel. I'll just put on his card that I've given the anti-tetanus." She went back to her desk, sat down, and was writing, when she felt rather than saw the two standing at the waiting-room door, the girl leaning against the door-frame, the boy against the door itself. They were both smoking.

"Smoking is not allowed in here, please."

"Oh? What's that ashtray doing there on that desk, then?"

"That's for the doctors. You can have a cigarette in the waiting-room but not in here."

They retreated, but the door of the waiting-room remained open and a strange smell permeated. Nurse Reynolds immediately recognized it—marijuana. That had got to be stopped, she thought, but the look on the faces of the girl and the boy as they sat looking at her deterred her for a moment from pressing the point. Still, she knew that it was her responsibility to insist that they did not smoke. She'd smelled that smell before, and on a patient—an unconscious patient. She plucked up her courage and walked to the waiting-room door.

"Please put those cigarettes out. I know that is not tobacco."

The boy, his leg crossed over his knee in a position similar to the girl's, his shoe resting on his dirty jeans, looked at her, took a deep pull on the cigarette, held his breath, closed his mouth firmly over the smoke, and after a moment said:

"Oh, so it's grass, is it? Had some, have you? Recognize it? Want to make something of it? I wouldn't. I can have friends in here in minutes. I've only got to get on the phone. Another thing—who's this Patel you were ringing? Don't want no Pakis to look after my mate. Haven't you got an English one?"

"Dr. Patel is a perfectly efficient and responsible doctor and he is on duty, and that is who your friend will have and he's lucky to have him." Anger at the criticism of the Casualty officer momentarily blotted out Reynolds's fears.

"Well, wait till he gets here. He'd better be good, that's all."

Reynolds looked towards the girl, and she too was dragging heavily on a thin cigarette.

At that moment the door into Casualty opened and Dr. Patel came in. He did not have to pass the two young people, as he came in by the side-door, for which Reynolds was grateful. She went back into Casualty, closing the waiting-room door behind her. She and the doctor went through and joined Nurse Andrews at the patient's side.

She removed the sterile green dressing-towel that she had put over the arm, and the doctor looked at the injury.

"That's not nice, Staff Nurse, it's a nasty injury. How did you get that, what happened?"

The boy on the couch opened his eyes and looked at him. The moment he saw the Indian doctor his look became guarded and hostile.

"Don't want no Injuns looking after me," he said. "Don't want no Pakis."

"I am not a Pakistani and I am going to look after you," said Dr. Patel coldly. He gently took hold of the boy's hand and moved the arm gingerly. The boy let out an exaggerated scream. At that scream the two burst in from the waiting-room, taking no notice of Staff Nurse Reynolds's stern "Go back and wait where you were."

"I told you we didn't want no Paki looking after him."

"Dr. Patel is well qualified to look after your friend. He will have to be admitted to the ward." Staff Nurse Reynolds signalled to Nurse Andrews to go and ring for a porter.

As Nurse Andrews put down the phone it rang. She answered it and then turned to her senior.

"Mrs. Haslemere has come and is in X-ray waiting. O.K.?"

Again Nurse Reynolds nodded and at that moment a porter came through, pushing a trolley erratically in front of him.

"Met Mrs. H. coming in. She said you'd got someone for X-ray."

Nurse Andrews caught hold of the end of the trolley and brought it up beside the patient, completely ignoring the girl and the boy, pushing them back to let the trolley through.

Dr. Patel and the two nurses lifted the boy onto the trolley. His arm was now in a sling. Nurse Andrews raised the back rest of the trolley at her senior's instructions and the boy leaned against it, only once opening his eyes and acknowledging his two friends.

"We're coming with you to see you're all right. We won't leave."

"Have you had anything to eat within the last hour or so?" It was Dr. Patel speaking, and the boy looked at him and then at the other two.

"When did we . . . What was it?"

The morphia that Reynolds had administered was already taking effect, easing the pain, making the patient feel slightly muddled and sleepy.

"Fish and chips," said the girl quickly, "about—ooh—about four hours ago, I suppose."

"Very well, then," said Patel.

The porter, a small and insignificant man, looked rather apprehensively at the two going down to X-ray with him. As he backed out of the Casualty door he knocked the side of the trolley against the doorway and the patient gave a yelp of pain. In a flash the boy came forward, grabbed the porter by his lapels and almost lifted him off the floor.

"Watch yourself, man," he said. "If you do that again I'll slit your bloody throat." The little porter put on a brave face.

"That'll do. I didn't do it on purpose. That'll do, son."

"Don't 'son' me, man," said the boy and to Reynolds's horror she saw he had a flick-knife in his hand.

"Put that away at once," she said, coming forward to the porter's aid. "Any more nonsense from you and I'll get the police. I'll go down to X-ray with these people." She looked at the porter reassuringly, then stopped as the Casualty officer spoke to her hesitatingly. It was as if his confidence had been shaken by the presence of these young hooligans.

"What do you think, Staff Nurse? X-ray and then to the ward? Shall we leave it till morning? No, I think not. I'll ring Mr. Harris," he ended lamely. He was quick to see the look of contempt on the girl's face as she said:

"You'd better, if he's your boss-man."

The trolley then disappeared with the porter, Staff Reynolds, the girl, and the boy. The outer waiting-room door shut behind them and Nurse Andrews was left with Dr. Patel. He reached towards the phone, then brought his hand back.

"I needn't phone yet, I suppose," he said.

"Don't take any notice of them. They're punks, they're nothing," said Nurse Andrews, and he looked up at her from where he was sitting at the desk.

"I know that," he said, "I know that all right, but that was cannabis, wasn't it? I could smell it and I said nothing. They make you fearful, these—They make you afraid. In Birmingham we got mugged, my brother and I, beaten up. Paki bashing, they called it. My brother got quite badly hurt. I took him back to the hospital, to Casualty, where I worked. His eye was cut, and he lost it. You think of that when these young people are around."

"I know," said Nurse Andrews. "I'm sorry about your brother. I didn't know." She hoped they'd get no more like that boy and girl in tonight, none of their mates coming in to see what was going on. She wondered how they'd behave when they got to the ward—when they were through X-ray. They'd had a bit of this kind of thing before, but they hadn't been as bad as this. There weren't many in their little town, but there were too many, she thought as she watched Dr. Patel at last summon up enough courage to pick up the telephone and phone the orthopaedic registrar for his advice.

CHAPTER 10

In her cottage Carmichael was not having a good night. The finding of Tibbles up the tree worried her. She hoped the cat wouldn't get flu. She was innoculated against it, but . . . She twisted and turned and then a rumble of thunder woke her up fully. The storm had almost died away but occasionally flashes of sheet lightning showed through her bedroom curtains. She got up and decided she would go downstairs and make tea.

She opened the back door while she waited for the kettle to boil in the kitchen. The smell of earth and wet grass came to her soothingly. She stood there in the very slight breeze in her night-dress and dressing-gown thinking of the stormlit scene she had left earlier that evening.

Was he dead? He had looked it. But that pulse . . . Should she have tried again, waited, and then tried again? Had she taken too much for granted when she'd driven away? Supposing he recovered? Had she done all the right things? She'd left the door open. Was that the right thing to do? Was it possible a man could get in front of his car and it run forward? Of course it was. In fact, she was nearly sure she had heard of an accident like that. She was worried, though, more worried than usual on such occasions. She gave herself the old familiar Carmichael shake and said to herself, Come on, come on, you know it's always all right.

The kettle clicked off behind her. She took down the tea caddy and put one tea-bag in the pot and poured on boiling water. As she did so, a crowd of memories came jostling back. Sister Jones, her mother—the rotten tea Jones always made. Christmas, Harry—Harry would now be sleeping beside his wife, Margaret Tarrant, now Margaret Maitland. That was terrible, she didn't want to think of that. Her thoughts turned almost with relief to Jack Sampson lying there. Yes, the heavy wheel of the car had gone over his chest. He must be dead, of course he must.

The two cats came down and walked out into the wet garden. When she had finished her first cup of tea, she called them back and after a moment they came obediently and she shut the kitchen door. She did not feel totally reassured, however. What else should she have done? She had to take the chance. Look at that man Abbott, he might have . . . but he'd died at once. His wife too had died. No, her luck always held. Mrs. Abbott could have rushed out of the house when she smelled the smoke, and he could have saved himself as he fell, but they hadn't. No, she was just being stupid.

She poured herself out another cup of tea and took it upstairs to bed and, after she had drunk it, switched off the bedside light. She tried, too, to switch her mind off like the electric light, but it wasn't easy. She turned on her side and gazed at the curtains, waiting for the next flash of lightning. One came and she thought to herself, If three more come then he's dead.

For a little while the square of window remained dark, then there was another flash. "One," Carmichael said loudly to herself. Almost at once there was another flash. "Two," she said. One more and there was no question, nothing to worry about. It was a long time before the next flash—there was practically no thunder now—then suddenly it lighted up the square of window—the third flash—and at last Carmichael was reassured.

The two cats leaped onto the foot of her bed. Carmichael fell into a dreamless sleep.

When she woke the next morning at the correct time, in spite of the fact that she had forgotten to set her alarm clock, apprehension flooded over her again. She remembered counting the flashes of lightning and thought how foolish she was. She couldn't wait to know whether he was dead.

She dressed, fed the cats, but could eat no breakfast herself.

At last she got into her car and drove along the road. She dreaded rounding the bend where the car had stood. Would it still be there? And the body? It could be, the traffic on this side-road was infrequent. She turned into the short stretch of lane where the car had stood last night. She visualized it vividly, but this morning it would look different because of the sunshine.

The stretch of road was empty. There was no car, no Jack Sampson. Carmichael felt compelled to pull into the side of the road just ahead of where the car had stood last night. She must look, she must check. Check what, she didn't know, but she must check.

She walked back, carefully avoiding the puddles, looking along the grass verge. She did not know what for . . . blood? The green grass gleamed in the morning sun still wet, but there was no blood.

At that moment a red car came round the bend and approached. The two women in the car looked at her and drew to a halt beside her. Carmichael felt her apprehension give way now to terror. What should she say if they asked her what she was doing? She recognized the woman who was driving. It was a Mrs. Pilcher who lived some way below her in the lane, and the other must be—she peered into the car, yes, she recognized her too—Sampson's wife.

The woman driving leaned out of the car window.

"It's Sister Carmichael, isn't it?" Mrs. Pilcher said pleasantly. Carmichael nodded. "What are you doing here?"

Was Mrs. Pilcher's voice suspicious? She looked white and strained as if she'd been up all night, as well she might, Carmichael thought.

"Yes, I saw something shining in the road. It looked like a . . ." The lie leaped to Carmichael's lips so easily.

Mrs. Pilcher turned and said something to her passenger and got out of the car.

"Where?" she asked. "It might be something belonging to poor Jack. He was killed here last night. We found him on the way home. It was awful."

"Killed? How?" Carmichael made her voice sound incredulous.

"His own car ran over him. He was there under the wheel, blood and everything. We were coming home from bingo, late, and we saw the car. She found him. We've had an awful night. They took him away, and the car."

Suddenly Mrs. Pilcher burst into tears and, fumbling in her pocket, brought out a crumpled handkerchief and blew her nose violently.

"I'm so sorry, so terribly sorry," said Carmichael. "I knew him well, of course. What a terrible thing to happen."

Mrs. Pilcher acknowledged Carmichael's remarks with a miserable nod of her head and a further blowing of her nose and wiping of her eyes.

"Something shining, you said?" She came back along the road, looking on the grass verge. Then suddenly she darted through the wet grass behind Carmichael.

"Look, here's what you saw." She had picked up a small object and she held it out to Carmichael. "It's his hospital badge. There's his name inside."

It was small, round, and silver, the pin open. It rested in the palm of Mrs. Pilcher's hand, shining. It would undoubtedly have caught anyone's eye if they had seen it in the sunlight. *If,* thought Carmichael. That her glib explanation had been proven was providential, proof that Jack Sampson's fate was justified.

"He was proud of that, always wore it, even off duty. I think I'll give it to her, shall I?"

"I should. Strange, I just saw something shining and stopped."

"Yes, lucky you did, it might never have been found and I know she'll like to have it. It may upset her but . . ." Mrs. Pilcher got back into her car. "We're going to fetch his things and see Mr. Wills and the police."

Carmichael went round the car to the passenger side. Helen Sampson wound down the window, and her red, swollen eyes met Carmichael's.

"Oh, it was horrible, Sister," she said thickly. "They say he didn't suffer, but I don't know . . . How can they really tell? He was crushed—his chest—there was blood . . . I found him. I nearly fell over him."

"Poor Mrs. Sampson. What a dreadful experience for you. I'm so sorry."

Helen Sampson started to weep again and Mrs. Pilcher leaned forward to speak to Carmichael.

"We must get on," she said. "Thank you for this." She held up the badge, started the engine, and they drove off.

Carmichael watched the car out of sight, then got into her own and realized that she felt rather dizzy and she was glad to sit down. After a second or so the feeling abated. She felt empty, as though everything she had just seen and the conversation she had just had was a dream.

The sunlit lane, the birds singing, the trees, the tangled hedgerow, the bright pools of water each side left by last night's rain appeared to her like a painting or a coloured photograph. Nothing moved. Then a bird dipped down to the road and started to bathe in one of the pools. Industriously it splashed, throwing the water into the air in bright droplets. Tibbles would have killed it, Carmichael thought—life is all death. She started the car and continued her drive to the hospital, primed with the knowledge that Jack Sampson was dead and would never trouble her or her nurses again.

CHAPTER 11

Carmichael arrived late at the hospital, so after she had changed, she took the lift up to her ward. It was then, in spite of its good beginning, that the morning started to go awry. The lift journeyed upwards in its jerky fashion, almost to her own floor, then stuck, and Carmichael was stranded about waist-high on her ward. She looked out in fury as, luckily, one of her nurses went by.

"Nurse, get the electrician, this lift has stuck again." She put up her hand and punched the button as Staff Nurse Miles had done, but nothing happened. The lift trembled a little, then was still.

"Oh, Sister, what a nuisance. Yes, I'll go and ring him," said the nurse and she went on through the swing-doors. After about five minutes the electrician came.

"Oh, Lord, not again. Sorry, Sister, but they're not closing the gates properly. I'll go and look." He disappeared down the stairs and soon came back again and said to Carmichael:

"Press the button now, Sister." Carmichael did and the lift rose to her own floor and stopped. She opened the doors.

"When is this lift going to be seen to? I've asked again and again. I just don't understand why in a hospital we have to have a faulty contraption like this—it's dangerous."

"I know it's difficult, Sister, but it's not really dangerous, not if everybody closes the doors properly and doesn't slam them behind them," said the young man. "It's just that people don't take enough care, they're in so much of a hurry, and then it doesn't make a perfect circuit, and of course—"

"Well, it should, there's no excuse whatever," said Carmichael as she closed the door behind her with a bang.

"There, you see. I don't think you've closed that door properly, Sister." The electrician opened the doors again and pushed the grille to more firmly. "See?"

"Well, it shouldn't happen and I wish to goodness they'd do something about it."

"I know, Sister, but the staff aren't really supposed to use it, you know. It's for the porters, for the trolleys, the patients from theatre and physio and X-ray. You know that, Sister, or you're supposed to."

"It's a good job somebody other than a patient was using it," Carmichael said witheringly as she walked away to her own wards.

Her Staff Nurse greeted her.

"Good morning Staff," said Carmichael, noting that the girl was anxious to speak, that obviously she had news to impart.

"What do you think, Sister, poor Jack Sampson, he was—"

"I know. I met his wife this morning on my way here. Now, do you think you could allow me to go to my office and start my work?"

Staff Nurse Minter looked deflated. "Well, I think it was awful. I mean, poor Jack, he was here yesterday talking to us."

"About the union, wasn't it?" said Carmichael and went into her office with the night Staff Nurse to receive the report, apologizing for her unusual unpunctual arrival.

"Quiet night, Staff Nurse?" she asked out of habit as she walked in and sat down. The nurse stood beside her, a book in her hand, and then sat down by the side of the desk. She proceeded to go through the patients one by one, but not before she had said rather querulously:

"Not particularly quiet, Sister, since you ask, not with the new patient we got in last night."

"Oh well, tell me about him when you get to him."

The girl started reading out the names and conditions of the men in the men's orthopaedic ward much as usual, until she came to the name Leo Kalinsky.

"This boy"—she looked up at Carmichael—"a right

yobbo." She looked down again at her report, and Carmichael commented coldly:

"That hardly comes into the night report, does it, Nurse?"

The girl murmured, "Sorry," and then went on: "Leo Kalinsky admitted at two-forty a.m., taken to the theatre, three-thirty a.m. Crushed right elbow—the injury caused by the limb being squashed between a car and a wall." She looked up again. "May I say, Sister, I believe this was done on purpose. They were having some kind of fight. That's all we could get out of him. They swear they don't know who the other boys were. Perhaps they don't." She looked down again.

"They?" said Carmichael. "Did he tell you all this?"

The girl nodded and went on. "Dr. Patel called in Mr. Harris. Dr. Patel felt he should get this one done and not put it on the end of the list. It was a very bad fracture. The X-rays are with the notes. Mr. Harris reduced the fracture to the best of his ability."

Carmichael looked at her and the girl said defensively: "They were Mr. Harris's own words, according to Dr. Patel. It was an awful mess, Sister."

"I see. Go on."

"Dr. Patel wrote up some sedation. It was quite an extensive op. The fracture was compound, part of the elbow sticking through the flesh. Mr. Harris said he doesn't know whether the disorganization of the joint was reduced completely. He hopes Mr. Dalby will look at the X-ray today."

"Well, I hope Mr. Harris was treated well on my ward?" said Carmichael.

"He didn't come down here. Dr. Patel came from theatre with the patient and that is what he said. He said it was quite a job."

Carmichael nodded and the nurse continued the rest of the report. The night otherwise had been quiet.

"Well, that doesn't seem to have been a very busy night," said Carmichael.

The nurse closed the report book with a bang.

"You could say that, Sister, except two of Kalinsky's friends came up here to wait for him to come down from the theatre, and that wasn't till after five this morning. They were here for ages, in the rest-room part of the time, where they played a radio loudly and, according to the nurses in Casualty, smoked cannabis down there. Here they demanded to see him and I couldn't keep them out. I got the night porter, but you know how small he is. He couldn't do anything. I've never, all the time I've been nursing, I've never had two people behave like this."

Carmichael sat, her back very straight. This was bad, this was something that might well have to be dealt with during the day. She felt quite able to deal with it.

"What are they like, this girl and boy?" she asked.

"The boy is just an ordinary sort of skinhead type. The girl, she's something else—purple lipstick, bright yellow hair, a real punk. Staff Nurse Reynolds from Casualty did ring me up to tell me what they were like. They had quite a time with them in Casualty. They threatened to break the place up, screamed at Dr. Patel that they weren't having a Pakistani. It was awful, Sister, it really was. What can you do in the middle of the night with only old Parker on? It was a wonder they didn't go up to the theatre and start something. I've heard of this happening in other hospitals, but well! I didn't expect it here."

Carmichael sat very still. This was something she'd have to think over. The thought of Jack Sampson was driven completely from her mind. She, like the night nurse, had heard of this type of youth getting onto the ward. Where was it? Liverpool? London? She couldn't remember, but she'd read it in the paper somewhere, and with some disquiet.

"They'll have to be disciplined. I can probably cope with these young people. Two of them, you say?"

"Just two, the girl and the boy. Doug, she calls him. I've forgotten what he calls her. Oh, I know, it was Jane. They may have other friends who are worse." She got up. "All right then, Sister?"

"Yes, thank you, Staff Nurse."

The nurse collected her cloak which she'd flung over the back of a chair and picked up a bag from beside it.

"Awful about Sampson, Sister, eh?"

Carmichael inclined her head. "Yes, yes, quite dreadful."

"Thank you then, Sister. See you tonight. I hope you have a quiet day." She looked meaningly at Carmichael.

"Oh, I shall, don't worry," said Carmichael and beckoned Nurse Minter across to her and asked, "Is Staff Nurse Miles on duty, Staff Nurse Minter?"

"He's on at two, Sister," said the nurse, looking at the rota, pushing the door of Carmichael's office slightly shut so that she could read it. "Comes on at two. Two to eight."

"I see," said Carmichael and proceeded to tell Staff Nurse Minter of the problems that might beset them, very sure, though, that her Staff Nurse would have heard most of it from the night nurse, and with embellishments.

CHAPTER 12

Leo Kalinsky opened his eyes and gazed round the ward. This was the second time he had waked up after having been taken to the operating theatre. The whole night was a kind of misty memory. He remembered being wheeled along a corridor with lights above him. He couldn't quite think where he was when these lights . . . It was something they'd given him. He remembered vaguely the theatre, then the anaesthetic and a high whistling noise in his ears—that's all, really.

His arm was hurting. He knew they'd given him something for the pain. Was it hours ago? He didn't know the time. He closed his eyes, wondering about Jane and Doug. Would they come and see him? Had they told his father? Had his father been sober enough to understand? Well, it didn't matter. He wondered too about his elbow. He supposed it was all right. He looked down. There was a plaster on his arm and it was bent across his chest. There was blood on the plaster. Well, they hadn't taken his arm off, anyway.

He dozed a little, then woke again and wondered about the blood on the plaster. Was it coming from inside? He supposed it must be. He didn't want to look at it, so he kept his eyes shut. Time went by, then there was a light touch on his arm, his good arm. He looked up. Standing at his bedside was a nurse. She looked small and pretty. Her face, completely devoid of make-up, was slightly flushed just over the cheekbones. Her eyes, dark-fringed and deep blue, looked down at him with slight anxiety. Her hair, he noticed, was golden. Although she tried to keep it severely back, little wisps strayed round her face.

"Are you all right? Does your arm hurt?"

Leo looked at her speculatively, as he did all girls.

"How can I bloody be all right after what's happened to me?" He attempted to move his right arm slightly and winced with pain. He felt giddy.

"Don't do that and don't swear," the nurse said with almost a mock severity because a smile accompanied the remark, and again he looked at her with narrowed eyes.

"Why shouldn't I swear? There's bloody well enough to swear about. Christ almighty."

"Now that won't make things better and, well, it often offends people, some people, especially if they're . . ."

". . . specially if they're what?"

"Well, religious, you know. Some of them are. Mr. Russell next to you, he is, for a start. Just cool it, eh?"

For some reason, and in spite of his pain, the girl made a smile appear on Leo's face which he didn't really intend.

"I see, all holy. Well, the sooner I get out of here the better. Can I have some dope?"

"You've had some, about half an hour ago. You can't have any more for a bit."

"It hurts." The boy sounded young and fretful and the nurse again put her hand sympathetically on his good arm and her fingers pressed it gently.

"I know, it will for a while, but it will get better, especially if you can relax, you know."

"Relax! Here? I could do a bit of relaxing if I had a . . ."

"Had a what?" asked the nurse, but Leo changed the subject hastily.

"Oh, nothing. What's your name?"

"It's Mavis Blake."

He looked at her hand. "M-m, thought you were making a pass at me."

She drew back from the bed, offended, and turned away.

Leo was sorry to see her go but he really wasn't used to dealing with dames like that. Anyway, he felt weary. He closed his eyes again and dozed off.

He had been sleeping when he felt a further pressure on his

arm. This time it was not quite so gentle. He roused himself to take in the new figure who stood beside his bed, clad in a dark blue dress with a black belt, a silver buckle on the front of it. She was angular with sandy hair matching the eyelashes round her washed-out eyes. Her mouth, thin and turned down at the corners, was nothing like the young, buxom girl's who had last spoken to him.

"I'm Sister Carmichael," the woman said. "I'm in charge of this ward. How are you feeling?"

"Not so bad," Leo mumbled.

"Good. I heard there was some trouble when you came in, trouble with your companions. If they're visiting again I hope they will behave themselves." Carmichael sorted through the letters she had in her hand. "No post for you, but then one could hardly expect there to be. Visiting time, as I expect you know is—But I won't bother you with it. I expect they gave you the book of instructions to give to your friends. What about your parents, have they been told?"

"I dunno, there's only me dad. Well, I expect the fuzz went to tell 'im, that is, if he wasn't too drunk to take it in. He usually is at night."

"I see."

Leo saw the woman at the side of his bed stiffen and he grinned inwardly. One in the eye for her, he thought. She'd probably run this ward for ever by the look of her. Maybe she was used to his kind and the old daddies like the one opposite. He reached forward to his locker to avoid the stare of her pale eyes and fumbled round till he found cigarettes and matches that he knew Jane had put in the locker last night. He was about to extract a cigarette with difficulty when Carmichael put up her hand admonishingly.

"No smoking at this time in the morning," she said. "You can smoke in the afternoon when you're more recovered."

"But I *want* to smoke now," Leo said.

Carmichael looked at him steadily. "No smoking until I tell you. You've had an anaesthetic, remember."

"I'm bloody well not likely to forget."

"And no swearing either, please, not in my ward."

"Oh, you own the bloody ward, do you? I mean the bloody ward belongs to you?" He felt suddenly ill and weary again. His arm ached and he was tired of talking to this woman. He relaxed against the pillows from which he had momentarily raised his head. He closed his eyes, his hand still clutching the cigarette and matches. He felt Carmichael standing there and decided to take the little nurse's advice—let it cool for a bit. He didn't feel like doing anything else. He felt Carmichael surprisingly gently remove the cigarette and matches from his hand and put them back in his locker and arrange the sheet comfortably across him. He did not open his eyes.

When he did at last open them again, she had gone. He turned his head and saw she was already three beds up the ward away from him talking to someone he couldn't see. He looked at her stiff, straight, navy-clad back and a little sneer came over his face. Then as the same nurse he had seen before went by he called out, "Hey."

She went over to him.

"What's for Sister Blister?" He inclined his head towards Carmichael, who was farther away still by now.

The nurse giggled appreciatively but belied the giggle by saying, "You must not speak about Sister Carmichael like that. Sister's all right. She keeps everything together, so you'd better watch it." The words accompanied by a curl of her pretty lips and a sparkle in her blue eyes placated his temper.

"My mates are coming this evening. You'll like them. They're bifferoos." He winced as he tried to move his arm slightly and the nurse went round and moved the pillows that supported the elbow.

"Never mind your friends, they may not get in this evening. Sister may think you're too poorly. You take it easy. This hurts, doesn't it? You just rest. You've got a nasty elbow there and you've had an operation."

"I've got a nasty nothing, I'm beautiful," he said, but the look of pain had not left his face. He still felt the twinge at the elbow going right up to the shoulder, and he couldn't suppress another grimace.

"You'd probably be better without visitors today. Anyway, what's a bifferoo?" she said.

Leo looked at her but did not answer her question.

"They'll bloody come anyway so she'd better be careful, your Sister. I'm not having any—"

"Please don't go on like that, it only tenses you up and makes the pain worse."

Leo looked at her. "What do you know about anything at your age?" he said grumpily and turned his head away so as not to see the effect of his words on the girl's smiling face. She turned away from him and he didn't open his eyes to watch her go.

Wait till they come, he thought, wait till they come. They'll . . . He felt a sudden need for revenge, revenge on anybody for what they had done to him. This bloody elbow. Suddenly it crossed his mind, what about bowling? This was his bowling arm. Oh well, maybe they'd make it all right, these medics, but that Indian wallah he probably didn't know his arse from his elbow. He started to doze again.

That evening, after Carmichael had gone off duty, Leo's father came to see him. The boy watched him weave his way up the ward after all the other visitors had arrived.

"What have they done then, boy, are they treating you all right? Want me to talk to them?" His father's voice was slightly thick and his breath reeked of beer, but he was unusually sober for this time in the evening. He stayed about ten minutes.

"Want anything, lad?" he asked, then got up to leave as Leo shook his head.

"Not unless you see Doug or Jane. They'll know what I want."

"Those punks!" His father started to shout and Leo hastened to quieten him down.

"All right, Dad, ease it. They'll come and they'll bring me anything I want."

"You'd be better off without them," muttered his father as he left the ward, hardly turning to look at his son.

Leo looked after him. Well, the visit had been better than he'd expected, really. His father drank so much that sometimes he was paralytic by this time. He sighed. The sharp movement he had made to watch his father go down the ward had made his arm painful.

The little fair-haired nurse appeared again at his bedside.

"Hurting?" she asked.

Leo looked up at her. "What d'you think?"

"You had a visitor," she said tentatively. "Who was it, your father?"

Leo nodded and closed his eyes again. He didn't want to talk about it. Suddenly he felt, for the first time in his life, ashamed.

"It hurts like hell," he said gruffly, motioning towards his elbow.

"I'll see if I can get you something for it." The nurse looked down at him, her eyes full of compassion, but compassion was something Leo Kalinsky did not want.

"Don't bother," he said.

The compassion in her eyes did not decrease and she touched him lightly on his good arm as she had before and said, "I'll see what Staff Nurse says," and turned before he had time to reply, walked down the ward and out.

Almost imperceptibly his shoulders shrugged. "Well, all right, then, do what you like," he said under his breath and turned his head away. He could have cried. He felt suddenly very alone. He wished that Jane and Doug would come, but as he turned towards the door he could see that the visitors were now going out and Jane and Doug had not come. He waited for the fair-haired nurse to come back.

CHAPTER 13

The following day was Carmichael's day off. She spent it pleasantly, weeding the garden—the two cats frolicking round her in the autumn sunshine—cutting the grass, collecting the windfalls from her apple trees, picking some asters for the cottage, and generally tidying up. The birds sang in her apple trees, it was peaceful and still warm during the day, though cool enough in the evening for her to light her fire. Her life felt rounded, complete, and she was contented.

Now and again she thought of Harry and what her life would have been like, but she was bound to admit in her own heart that she wouldn't have fitted. It would have, perhaps, been a disaster for him and, after all, he had been the only one who mattered. Lately she'd thought of him less and less. Only when depression overcame her had his face appeared in front of her eyes. Sometimes in the evening when she felt lonely she looked up from the television, glanced round her little room, then thought of him. She would sometimes see him in her memory's eye, his white stick, his handsome—no, beautiful—face, his sightless eyes. She could remember how they always sought her face when she spoke, but time made it less painful and her bouts of depression had become less frequent.

Jack Sampson hardly came into her mind at all. It had always been the same, she thought, when she had done something that she had had to do. It merely made her feel free, more adult. He had been dead two days now. Probably Mrs. Sampson would be getting over it a bit, be glad she was rid of the little creep. Anyway, it meant that for the moment her nurses were safe from being wheedled and cajoled into doing something no nurse should do.

Carmichael wondered idly how many of them had joined his union. She thought probably he'd managed to persuade quite a few. She'd do her best to get them back to the College of Nursing. But some of them didn't think the College did enough. They thought another union would have more clout—that was the word they used. Well, perhaps they were right, but it wasn't money one nursed for, thought Carmichael. Perhaps Jack Sampson would get his values right now that he was hustled into another world.

These thoughts made her rather more comfortable than anything else. She purposely kept away from doing much in the front garden in case Mrs. Pilcher should drive Mrs. Sampson by. They would have to pass the cottage if they were going to town and Carmichael didn't want to see them.

By the evening Carmichael, her mind never far away from her work, wondered if those two awful creatures had come to see the boy with the elbow. Well, she hoped her nurses would be able to handle them. She would see that they gave her no trouble, but she did wonder about this evening. Staff Nurse Miles was on duty and he wasn't the strongest personality—but strong enough, perhaps. After all, he had stood up to Jack Sampson during the incident at the lift. This brought back the memory of the unpleasant treatment she had received in the secretary's office. Well, perhaps he wouldn't have so much to say about who should report to whom now Sampson was dead.

She decided to dismiss the whole thing from her mind. She didn't want to think of the past. She concentrated on what she was doing. At that moment she was polishing a small piece of furniture in her sitting-room, something she loved to do. She found the smell of the polish pleasant and the action of polishing soothing. She looked at her watch. Nearly news time. The day had flown by.

She didn't usually mind being alone, she reflected—she found her own company good company—but quite suddenly she had one of her bouts of loneliness. They could come at any moment. Even when she was feeling good, they could come and block the good feeling out. She crossed the sitting-room and switched on the radio.

She went to the door and called in the cats and they came bounding across the now-damp grass towards her through the dusk of the early evening. Tibbles made a chirruping noise as she always did when she came in, and Torty followed, slightly more sedate, behind her. Carmichael closed the back door and locked it, securing the little bolt on the cat-flap too, so that they couldn't go out until their final walk just before she went to bed.

She changed the radio for television and sat down. Then she decided her feet felt rather cold. She smiled to herself even while she thought this, because she wondered if it was just an excuse to light her fire—it was such a comfort. She struck a match. Soon the wood and paper caught and the room seemed to come alive. She went upstairs and found her winter slippers and popped them on her feet. This slightly augmented her depression, to think that winter was coming, and dark nights. The winter evenings, of course, were more lonely than the summer. Wherever she was she had never liked drawing the curtains. Even in her old flat there had been something about it that was isolating, not like summer when you could go out in the garden and walk around and enjoy it. However, she must stop these gloomy thoughts, and she went and sat down again in front of the television.

What should she have for supper? She'd had quite a good lunch, so just a sandwich would do. Suddenly she saw in front of her endless suppers—endless sandwiches and baked beans on toast or bacon and egg—but what was more to the point was that they would always be alone. As if to comfort her, Tibbles jumped on her lap. She stroked the cat abstractedly. Always alone. Well, perhaps one day . . . but she didn't think so. She picked up her handbag, took out her compact and snapped it open and looked at herself. In the reflected light of the television she looked pale and her lashes almost non-existent. Should she use mascara? You need more than mascara, more than looks, even. You need—sex appeal. But what was sex appeal?

She got up and began to walk about the room, moving an ornament here and an ashtray there, though the ashtrays were never used. She was thinking about the indefinable quality of the young nurses at the hospital, their long glances at the doctors, even when they were handing them notes. She'd seen those looks so often, eyes meeting and holding for a minute. It wasn't exactly flirting, it was just a conscious understanding of the difference of their sex. Why did she never, never seem able to give that same look? Why did she never receive it? The upward glance . . . Mr. Dalby slipped into her mind suddenly. Mr. Dalby was attractive, and yet when he looked at her his glance never lingered; but it stopped at the physiotherapist, or a new young nurse. What was it? What was it that she hadn't got? She sighed.

Shut up, she said loudly to herself. It was no use thinking like that. You just had to accept what you were and, after all, she had certain powers, no one could deny that. She was a fixer of things. She must take comfort from that. No one would know—but *she* knew. She walked restlessly into the kitchen, then before she could start to prepare supper her feet took her back again into the sitting-room. It was no use. One thing did not make up entirely for the other. She leaned for a moment with her forehead against the window, looking out at the now almost dark garden. Suddenly in her imagination she felt Harry's warm strong arm about her. Her eyelids reddened and she felt the tears pricking behind her lids. She fumbled in her pocket, took out a tissue and wiped her eyes so vigorously that her eyelids stung. She blew her nose, then turned round determinedly.

"Come on, Tibbles, come on Torty, din-dins," she said. She walked through into the kitchen followed by the two cats and started to open a tin for their meal. After all, she had rid the hospital of an agitator—that surely was better even than the ability to flirt?

Then she realized that she felt hungry after all. She would

have bacon and egg for supper, not sandwiches. The television blared in the room behind her. Though it had been switched on, she had hardly noticed the news or what had followed. Stupid—she thought—waste of electricity. She turned back, went into the other room, and was about to switch it off when the local newscaster stopped her:

"A fatal car accident in Howgate Lane was responsible for the death of hospital porter Jack Sampson, well known in the district. He was—"

Carmichael switched it off. That was done, she was not interested and did not want to hear any more about it.

CHAPTER 14

The next morning Geoff Miles had a lot to tell Carmichael about Leo Kalinsky and his friends.

"Oh, they've come and made a complete nuisance of themselves." They'd arrived in the morning. "Everything happened, Sister," he complained. "At ten o'clock Leo puts on the radio. I didn't know he'd got one. He must have hidden it in the locker. I went and said he wasn't to do that. He could use his earphones and the proper hospital radio. But he wouldn't turn it down or off."

"Didn't you make him?" asked Carmichael incredulously, but Geoff had merely shaken his head and said it was impossible to tell him anything.

"Then, these two came, these punks. I'd heard about them. They were the ones who'd made such chaos in Casualty. They behaved disgustingly. They started to smoke, Leo as well, so I went and forbade them, and the boy spat on the floor right at my feet." Staff Nurse Miles went off into his usual "I've never been treated like this before in all my life" routine, which he was rather apt to do, and Carmichael tried to calm him down.

"Well, we'll just have to get one of the porters up next time. If they don't behave they can't come in."

"You try and keep them out, Sister. I tried when Mr. Dalby was here."

"When . . . what?" said Carmichael, scandalized.

"Mr. Dalby and Mr. Harris and Dr. Patel came up to see Leo Kalinsky because he was complaining so much about the arm. They had to take the plaster off. You know how those elbows swell, and he's just in the collar and cuff now. It's got to be plastered again but the wound looks all right and his temperature is normal. They wouldn't go out when the Consultant was there. Mr. Dalby said very politely to them, 'Will you please leave while I examine this patient?' They did move over to the other side of the ward, and that's all. Then while we were all there behind the curtains the girl stuck her head through and said, 'What are you doing to 'im?' That was just because he'd made a bit of a fuss when we took the plaster off. Nothing much, you know, but of course they saw the porter come in with the shears and . . . Well, I couldn't get them out, Sister, and they're coming again this afternoon."

"Well, they have a right to come if they behave," said Carmichael.

"I know, Sister, but it might be better to have them when other visitors aren't here. Heaven knows what they'll do or say. They do as they like and they say anything they like. Have you seen her? Wait till you do. She's just too much, she really is."

Staff Nurse Miles was obviously rattled.

"Another thing," he said, "they came up in the lift and got stuck and I had to get the electrician. I daren't touch those lifts now after the way . . . well, poor old Sampson told me off. Remember?" Carmichael nodded. "I managed to find the lift door that was not properly shut by going downstairs three flights and got them out while the electrician was looking at it. When they left they tried to wrench open the lift doors. The lift wasn't at the floor and I told them so but that didn't stop them. They punched and pulled at the doors and banged on the button. Eventually the lift came up and they went down in it. I hoped it would stick half-way between two floors. I felt like leaving them there if it did."

"Don't worry, I'll cope with it. I'm perfectly able to," said Carmichael, and as she spoke a positive blare of pop music came from the men's ward.

"There you are," said Staff Nurse Miles, but Carmichael did not answer him until she was out of her office and on the way to the men's ward. Then she turned round.

"I can cope with it," she said and walked along the row of beds. Two men spoke to her as she went by.

"For goodness' sake, Sister, make that young bugger turn that thing off," said one old man, and the other man backed him up.

Carmichael looked reprovingly at both of them. "Language, language, Mr. Beecham. Not on my ward, please," she said.

She arrived at Kalinsky's bed. He had a small transistor radio on the pillow by his ear. The noise was deafening and Carmichael had to shout to make herself heard.

"Shut that off straight away, please," she said.

Leo Kalinsky looked up at her and his eyes widened. "No, I like it. Helps the pain in me arm. Bloody painful me arm is."

"So I've heard in my report, and Mr. Dalby has been here to help you and I believe was extremely rudely treated by your friends."

"Oh, get lost, will you," said the boy, turning his head away from her.

Carmichael picked up the radio before Leo Kalinsky had a chance to see what she was doing. She switched it off and looked levelly at him.

"I'm confiscating this. You can have it when you go home," she said and turned to leave the bedside.

"If you take that away from me you'll regret it, Sister!" Leo Kalinsky's voice was low and cold. He was looking at her, the glittering eyes showing only through the slits of his lowered lashes. "You'll regret it, I promise you."

"Really," said Carmichael just as coldly, "then I'm afraid I'll have to regret it, won't I. If you had behaved reasonably and thought about the other patients who do not wish to listen to this racket you would not have had it confiscated."

The boy, his eyes not leaving her face, put his hand in the locker and brought out a packet of cigarettes and matches.

"No smoking either at this time," said Carmichael.

"Oh, Christ!" said the boy and Carmichael calmly took both cigarettes and matches from his hand and put them on the top of the transistor.

"I will give you these back when it is smoking time."

"It's just like being in a bloody school or bloody Borstal, that's what it is."

"Yes, it is, and I'm sure you will have had experience of the latter," said Carmichael. "Naughty boys get punished just like in school."

"You old cow. A paper hat on your head makes you think you're a bloody dictator," Leo shouted at her as she walked away.

"Be quiet, you foul-mouthed little yob," Mr. Beecham shouted, and several other patients joined in.

"All right, Mr. Beecham, I can handle this."

As she made her way down the ward she heard the old man say: "You wait till you get your next injection. You'll get a needle with a hook on it. They save those for the likes of you."

Carmichael permitted herself a slight smile and pretended not to have heard the remark. One of two of the patients clapped as she left the ward when they noticed the radio in her hand. This also she ignored.

CHAPTER 15

Leo Kalinsky's visitors did not arrive until nearly the end of visiting time. Carmichael had had a busy afternoon, interviewing relatives, giving them progress reports on their uncles or fathers or mothers. She sat down for a few minutes in her office waiting for the time when she could tell her nurses to collect the flowers and ring the visitors bell indicating it was time for them to leave.

She watched the girl and boy enter the ward. Everything Staff Nurse Minter had said about the girl was true. She was accompanied by the boy, whose shaven head made him look very like Leo Kalinsky. They did not glance in her direction.

Carmichael rose, when she judged they would have walked about half-way up the ward, and watched from the door. They gave loud whoops when they saw Leo, which made the other visitors look up. Carmichael frowned. They went to either side of the bed and the girl pulled out the long stool and sat down. The boy sat on the locker on the opposite side and they started to talk animatedly, but Carmichael didn't see anything pass from the visitors to the patient in the way of cigarettes or anything else. She returned to her office. She felt slightly tired. Reaction from Jack Sampson, she supposed. She always got that, first the elated, satisfied feeling, and then this strange disorientation. Then confidence ebbed back. However, she couldn't think about that now. She pulled the drug book towards her, which she was checking, and for the moment forgot about the two characters who had caused so much trouble. She was soon to be reminded. A man's voice rose angrily. She jumped up and went into the men's ward.

"No, you little sod, leave that alone. It hurts my leg when you move it."

Carmichael hurried up the ward to where the skinhead was fiddling about with some weights hanging from a man's leg at the end of the bed.

"Oh, I see. I thought it was some form of torture." The boy set the weights swinging and Carmichael reached his side white with anger.

"Don't touch that apparatus! You'll hurt the patient. It will cause his leg to—Get away from it, do you hear?"

The boy did not move, but stood with the cord of the extension which supported the weights between his fingers. After a second or two he let go, but twanged the cord with his fingernail.

"Who are you? You the Sister? The one who's nicked Leo's noise-box and his fags? Just give them back, or else I might"—he gripped the cord of the patient's extension more firmly—"I might just—Now, what would be the best thing to do?"

His other hand went into his pocket and he brought out a knife, flicked it open and stroked the blade against the cord.

The white-haired man in the bed, a man of about sixty, looked anxiously at Carmichael and then said, "Leave it alone, you little bastard."

The boy turned toward the man in the bed. "I should be quiet if I were you, grandad. I don't mean no harm to you. I just want my mate's transistor back and his ciggies. I'm not having any nonsense from this bitch here, so will yer get them or will yer not?" He looked toward Carmichael. "P'raps you've taken them home to keep for yerself. That's how you get things. That's what they used to do to us in school. 'This is confiscated,'" he went on in a high falsetto voice, "'this is confiscated, I'm afraid. You can't have it, not until you leave.' And did you get it? No, the teachers took more things than anyone knew about, I can tell you. We're not fools, yer know. Come on, I want that trans back." He ran the blade of the knife across the cord gently, but it was enough to make the man in the bed look towards Carmichael even more anxiously.

"Give it 'im, Sister, there's a good 'un. I don't want these weights to fall on the floor and me leg—It'll hurt it, won't it? Give it 'im back. After all, it's only a radio."

Carmichael looked towards Leo's bed. The girl had turned towards her and was watching, the purple lips split into a smile.

"I'd get it, Sister, I'd give it 'im," she said quietly. " 'E'll do it, believe me. Doug couldn't care bloody less—really."

Leo called out, "Come on, get me trans. I won't say another word, neither will he. We could do a lot in here, yer know. I couldn't, not now, but I will be able to later, so you watch yerself."

At that moment, Nurse Minter came up to Carmichael. "Shall I get a porter, Sister?"

Carmichael shook her head. "No. Get the transistor and the cigarettes from my office and give them to the patient."

It was a climb down but she couldn't let him cut the extension, and by the boy's look she could tell he would do it. He would do anything.

Staff Nurse Minter hurried away and came back with the radio and put it together with the cigarettes and matches on the bed by the side of Leo's good hand.

"There you are," she said, and Leo looked at Minter and grinned.

"Thanks a bundle," he said. "She's all right," he said to Jane, indicating Minter. "She ain't done nothing. It's that one there."

The boy who was standing by the other patient's bed snapped his knife closed and put it in his pocket. "Don't do that again, don't take anything from him again or you'll be sorry."

As he walked back to Leo's bed again the transistor blared out and the other visitors and patients watched the scene in some trepidation. One or two winced at the noise the radio made.

Carmichael did not say another word but walked out of the

ward into her office, picked up the telephone, and within a few moments the hospital secretary arrived.

"What is it?" he asked, but he needed to inquire no more when he heard the noise coming from the men's ward. "Good Lord, Sister, can't you stop them from making that noise?"

"Perhaps you'd like to try," Carmichael answered frostily. She and the hospital secretary were hardly on friendly terms. He looked into the ward, saw the two black-clad figures, and listened to Carmichael's description of the scene before he came to the ward.

"All right, I'll get Maynard," he said. Carmichael nodded.

Maynard was the porter who handled the linen and heavy supplies, a big, hefty man who appeared to be afraid of nothing. The secretary used her telephone and again within minutes the swing-doors parted and a large man, his grey coat flapping open, came in and walked towards Carmichael's office.

"What's on, then?" he asked.

"Trouble with some yobbos in there." Mr. Wills waved his Biro towards the ward.

The porter grinned. "What you want done, then?" He laughed at the blare of the music. "Ah, one of those."

"Two of those, a girl and a boy. The boy threatened to cut one of the extensions. They're dangerous young people. He has a knife."

"Which of 'em hasn't?" said Maynard, completely unmoved. "What d'you want done to 'em?"

"I want them evicted from the ward and I don't want them here again in this hospital. They can come back again if they're going to behave themselves, but not unless. That's the message," said the hospital secretary pompously. At that moment the bleep in his pocket sounded. He took it out, listened, then replied, obviously with some relief, "Yes, all right, I'll come straight away. No, I hadn't forgotten." He turned to Carmichael testily and said, "You could have rung for Maynard yourself, you know."

"Oh, really! And be told I was employing the wrong man

for the job again, I suppose. I would rather leave that to you, if you don't mind." Mr. Wills obviously took the point and turned on his heel and left the ward abruptly. Carmichael heard the lift gate clang. He was gone, glad to be out of the scene, no doubt.

Maynard turned to her with another wide grin, raising his big red fist. "Can't see 'em tackling this, not even his nibs, can you?"

Carmichael gave him one of her frosty smiles. "Go and have a word with them. You may be able to make them see sense."

"Not like you not to be able to keep them under, Sister," said Maynard, and he ambled off into the ward, his big form nearly filling the doorway as he went through. Carmichael followed.

"Well, me laddo, making trouble, eh? That won't do, will it. What 'ave you got 'ere, then?" He picked up the radio that was still blaring, switched it off, and slipped it into the pocket of his grey coat.

"Leave that alone."

Doug got up and his hand went toward his pocket, but before he could reach it the porter had taken hold of the back of his collar and pinioned his arms back.

"Naughty, naughty," Maynard said and started to propel the boy towards the door, still holding him by the collar and clutching his wrists behind him in his huge hands. He turned to the girl and looked her up and down.

"My, my, we've got a smart one here. You'd better come too, ducks, don't you think?" he said. The girl got up to follow him and turned towards Leo. At that moment the bell sounded for the visitors to depart. Everybody rose and started towards the door. Still held in a vice-like grip, the collar of his shirt twisted like a garotte, Doug could not move, but his face was contorted, red with rage. The girl followed behind him, looking somehow incongruous. The porter, holding the boy in front of him, marched him towards the door, followed by the girl. As she left Leo's bedside she turned round and said in a loud voice:

"Don't worry, don't worry, ducky, we'll get even. We'll make the buggers suffer, don't you worry. You just look after yourself. See you."

Leo waved rather feebly with his good arm and watched them as they left the ward.

Once outside the ward the big porter let go of the boy's collar but still kept hold of his arms. His hand dived into the boy's pocket and he took out the knife.

"Dangerous weapon. What would the fuzz say? Shall we ring 'em up and ask 'em to come and have a little talk with you?" He looked toward Carmichael. "What do you want me to do, Sister? Boot 'em down the stairs, or what?"

Carmichael looked undecided for a moment.

"What would the police do?" she asked Maynard. He grinned back at her.

"Oh, slap their wrists, I suppose. Can't do much. There would be plenty of witnesses if he was threatening violent behaviour but . . . I should let 'em go. If they come back I'll deal with them. I'll be here, don't worry. Here, you'd better have this." He took the little radio from his pocket and gave it to her, then gave her the knife.

"You're not always on duty, though, are you?" The boy spat out the words.

"No, I'm not, but I mostly am at visiting times. If I see you around, even in the town . . . well, you know what I mean?"

Maynard gave the boy a push towards the doors, the girl followed saying nothing, but Carmichael noticed her hands were clenched so that the knuckles showed white. Suddenly as Maynard and the boy disappeared to the stairs and she was about to follow she turned to Carmichael.

"You'll live to regret this, Sister whatever your name is. We don't like being humiliated. And you treat Leo right. We'll be back, and as for you, you'd better watch out. You'll be in for trouble."

Carmichael ignored her and went back into the ward to reassure the patients. She had a word with the man whose extension they had threatened to cut. She went round soothingly but still trembling with rage inside. How could she . . . What could she . . . ? People shouldn't treat her like this, it was dangerous. They didn't realize that but, well—when they came back . . . She'd think again about it and if their behaviour got any worse, well, they were the ones who had better look out.

CHAPTER 16

After Maynard had escorted the girl and the boy out of the ward, Carmichael did a full round, seeing every patient in both wards. They all seemed to want to speak to her about the incident and tell her what they thought of it. In the women's ward they heard the radio blaring out and also the rumpus that went on, and in the men's they had seen everything. After she had done this she decided to go to the dining-room for a quick cup of tea. She was off at six and didn't usually bother, but she felt more shaken than she had realized.

When she returned to the ward, time went quickly and it was soon six o'clock. Dr. Patel had come up to do a round and Carmichael had found him talking with Staff Nurse Minter outside the men's ward when she came back from the dining-room. She disliked this. She felt Minter was telling him about the afternoon's occurrences and of course, being mixed up with Casualty, he was interested. Carmichael broke into the conversation.

"Do you want to do a round, Dr. Patel?" she asked.

"Yes, just before I go off. I have to go out this evening and Dr. Manning is standing in for me."

Carmichael signalled to a nurse to bring the note trolley. It was not usual to do a round at this time, but she felt rumours of what had happened had gone round the hospital, as they usually did—almost, she felt, sometimes before they actually happened—and Dr. Patel would want to know more. Well, now he had said he wanted to do a round, he could do so. They proceeded, Carmichael mentioning the few things she had wanted to tell him. It was not the same as taking Mr. Dalby, or even the registrar, Mr. Harris, round. The whole thing was quick and informal, and after about twenty minutes Dr. Patel had gone.

At six Carmichael handed over to Staff Nurse Minter, and Minter, after the report was finished, said tentatively:

"What if they come back when Maynard is off?"

"Well, you'll just have to cope with it, won't you, Staff Nurse," said Carmichael. She herself didn't know what she would do if Maynard was not around for their next visit, but she could not deal with it now. She was worried about the cats. A long stint of duty from early morning till six at night always worried her. She didn't like leaving them for so long. She was always anxious.

"What about the radio?" Staff Nurse Minter asked. It was standing on the top of Carmichael's file in her office.

"Don't give it back to that boy. All right?"

Staff Nurse Minter nodded rather dismally. She could see difficulties ahead. Carmichael could see them too, but anyway . . .

"Staff Nurse Miles is on," she said. "You've got him to back you up if you need him."

"Oh, him," said Minter disparagingly, and at that moment Miles came through the door.

"Going off duty, Sister?" he asked as Carmichael raised a hand to him. He was junior to Minter, so he did not need a report.

"There you are," Carmichael said. "You'll be all right with a man on the ward. I'm glad he's here. Anyway, they may not come back tonight."

"Yeah, I suppose so. All right, Sister," said Minter and, as Carmichael got up to go to the changing-room, "I'll be all right, don't you worry."

Carmichael looked at her and didn't answer. Much as she cared for her ward, her mind, at the moment, was on her cats. She went through the swing-doors, looked undecidedly towards the lift, then decided to go down the stairs.

Once she was changed out of her uniform and in the car the incident on the ward became more distant. She slipped into the gear of her own life, thinking with pleasure of returning to her cottage, the cats waiting, waiting to be fed, she thought wryly. Where their love of her and love of food divided she didn't wish to think about. They loved her because she was the provider—that was enough.

It was not until she got into the lane where Jack Sampson's car had stood that she was conscious of the noise of an exhaust behind her. She looked in her mirror and saw two black-clad figures on a motor bike. They resembled Leo Kalinsky's two friends, but then they all looked alike, these young people, and the two black-visored helmets made them look like something from outer space. They slowed up slightly in the narrow lane as she drove towards her cottage and signalled that she was going to the right up the path that led to her garage. She drove in and as she did so the motor bike behind her roared even more loudly and accelerated away up the lane. Carmichael wondered where they were going. There were only a couple of houses beyond her cottage. One was Jack Sampson's and the other was Mrs. Pilcher's. The two figures had reminded her of —But that was silly.

She got out of her car and walked round from the garage to her front door. As she did so, she heard the noise of the motor bike coming back, but as neither of the helmeted heads turned in her direction she thought they must have taken a wrong turning. Many cars did that round here. They thought it was a fork leading somewhere, not realizing that it led farther out into the country and to a small pot-holed treacherous track.

She dismissed them from her mind and went into her cottage and called the cats. To her relief they came almost instantly. She was always haunted by a slight fear that they might get out into the fields and be attacked by something. But no, they were there, purring and welcoming her.

CHAPTER 17

The next day was the orthopaedic operating list and Carmichael and her staff had too busy a time to think of Leo in particular or his friends. It was not until two hip replacements had been safely returned from the operating theatre, put back to bed, and a nurse left by the side of each that Carmichael had a moment to go into her office, sit down, and draw up the daily report from the pile of books on the side of her desk in order to make notes of the operations.

It was then that she noticed the radio was no longer standing on the top of her file as it had been the night before. She called out to Geoff Miles, who was passing:

"That boy Leo's radio, where is it? He's not to have it back, you know."

Miles made a face. "Not to have it back . . . They came in yesterday evening, those two, took it out of your office, and gave it to him. I had to tell him off twice for blaring it out. I said they were to take it home with them. I don't know whether they did or not."

Carmichael was furious. "Why did you let them take it back? He's got the earphones, he can use those. How dare they come into my office! Why did you let them?"

"You should hear what he said about hospital radio, Sister. I couldn't stop them. I tried to," said Miles.

"Right," said Carmichael and got up and walked briskly to Leo's bedside.

"Where is your radio?" she asked.

"In me locker and there it's going to stay, so don't try anything."

Leo was feeling better now, getting less pain from his elbow.

He was sitting on the side of the bed, his legs swinging. He was not allowed to walk about the ward with his arm unplastered. It was now in a sling in a collar and cuff, as it was called in hospital. Another plaster was due to be put on today after the operating list when the arm had been re-X-rayed.

"Give it to me," said Carmichael, and the boy shook his head, his mouth stubborn.

"I wouldn't touch that radio, Sister," he said. "I haven't put it on—Well, I did last night just for a minute, just to get your stupid Staff Nurse in a lather. I don't want it here. Jane or Doug can take it tonight. I want more cigarettes, though. I'm fed up with this place. Can I go home after I've had my plaster?"

"We'll see," said Carmichael, although she had been told by Mr. Dalby that after the arm was replastered, providing the X-ray was satisfactory, the boy could go home.

"Well, I'm going anyway once it's done. I'm not going to hang around here. I hate this bloody place."

"Don't use language like that in my ward. I've told you about that before," said Carmichael. "And I warn you, if your friends behave in any way that I or my staff think is incorrect, they will not be allowed in to see you." The boy looked at her, his face really evil, yet with a smile on it that Carmichael could not understand.

"I wouldn't do that, Sister, really I wouldn't. You've done enough, you know. Jane and Doug, they've got friends and they might bring 'em along. What d'you think you'd do if six of 'em came? Your porters—well, that one heavy, what could he do? And the rest—they're not all strong men of Britain, are they? I wouldn't really, I wouldn't. If Doug gets mad he—"

At that moment a patient was wheeled into the ward—another hip replacement, the third, more than Carmichael was used to having on one list, but they were trying to reduce the interminable waiting list and were using two theatres, and the registrar was working in one and Mr. Dalby in the other.

Carmichael turned away from Leo at the moment. He was unimportant. She went up to the trolley on which lay the unconscious man, the drip stand swinging slightly as the porter and nurses backed it alongside the bed.

Leo got up, moved over and looked at the unconscious man, then at the drip suspended by his side.

"Hate to have that pulled out, wouldn't you? It might make things a bit dodgy for the old geyser, eh?"

"Get back to your bed." Carmichael's voice was shrill. The very thought of anyone doing such a thing, even threatening to do it, sent her pulse rate racing and her white face and compressed thin lips had an effect even on Leo, for he turned away and made towards his own bed, but threw over his shoulder as he did so:

"Watch it, then. Forbid them the ward? They've a right to go anywhere. We pay for this dump and your salary. You saw Doug, you saw Doug with that knife."

Geoffrey Miles at the head of the trolley said to Carmichael:

"Don't worry, Sister. Last night Douglas whatever his name is was flashing that knife about again in the ward. It frightened the patients a little, but not much. They thought he was bluffing, and so did I."

"Bluffing!" Leo said as he went and sat down on the locker by his bed. "Bluffing. You don't know our gang, you just don't know them."

Carmichael ignored him and drew the curtains round the bed while the porter and nurses gently lifted the patient.

They could not behave like this in a hospital. Carmichael wondered if she should report them again to the hospital secretary or to Miss O'Donoghue, say they needed the police here, do something to protect her patients. But then she got so little co-operation. She walked out of the ward leaving Geoff Miles to cope with the patient and found Miss O'Donoghue standing in her office.

She smiled as Carmichael approached. "Busy morning, Sister?" she asked, although she knew full well that the orthopaedic operation list always made a busy morning.

Carmichael merely nodded, but her preoccupied look and white face caused Miss O'Donoghue to look at her curiously.

"Anything the matter?" she asked.

"Oh, it's just that boy and girl. You know, the ones who gave trouble in Casualty. Well, they caused a bit of trouble here last night. It's not the first time. Staff Nurse Miles was on. I suppose it helped to have a man on duty, but, really, if they bring more friends, as Leo Kalinsky suggests they might, I don't know what we'd do. I don't know how we'd control them."

"Neither do I. They've had this in other hospitals in bigger towns. I just don't know what the answer is. Get the police, I suppose, but it's upsetting for the patients. Something ought to be done but I don't know what."

"No, and I don't know who to report it to."

"Why me, of course," said Miss O'Donoghue rather tartly. "Don't go direct to Mr. Wills again like you did over the lift. Oh, he told me about it—proper channels—you know him. I'll see what I can do. Perhaps . . . What we really want is a bigger establishment of porters, somebody who can cope with this kind of thing. If we get more of it, it's no use talking about cuts."

They went on to talk about the cases that had come back from the theatre and the ones that were still to go. The matter of the unwelcome visitors who would probably be in this evening left their minds.

"Has the lift been all right?" Miss O'Donoghue asked.

Carmichael looked at her again with that slightly preoccupied look. "The lift? Oh yes, for once it has behaved itself fairly well. There was a slight bit of trouble when we took it up to the theatre. It stopped about six inches below the floor, but we had a light patient on the trolley so we managed it. When are they going to put the new lift in?" Carmichael asked.

"Well, good news, but not such good news for the theatre. They'll have to do minors only or else manhandle the patients up and down the stairs. They reckon they're going to start them next week or the week after."

"I've heard that before," said Carmichael.

"Too true, so have I," said Miss O'Donoghue. "However it

might be true this time. It's the money, I suppose, or else getting it, the lift, I don't know. The workings of a hospital, my dear, you know what they're like. Where a friend of mine works they have been going to build a new hospital for twenty-five years and they haven't started yet. Generations of nurses have trained and gone hearing about the place and how wonderful it's going to be, but it's never materialized. What goes on there at the top makes you laugh, really. I guess it's the non-practical types that sort of rise upwards."

"Like scum," said Carmichael.

"Well, that's a bit," said O'Donoghue, laughing, "but I suppose I see what you mean. You'd better not let the administrative staff hear you say anything like that or you'll never get there."

Carmichael looked at her coldly. "Oh yes, I will," she said. "But when I get there there will be more done."

"What do you mean? Do you mean that I'm not—?"

"Oh no, of course not," said Carmichael suddenly weary. "It's just that the administrators higher than us are the ones that don't do anything, just talk. If they spent the time seeing to the new lift that they spend talking, things would get done."

"Too true," said Miss O'Donoghue again, and as Dr. Patel walked into the ward, still in his theatre gown, her face broke into a smile. It always did when she saw a man, thought Carmichael, as Miss O'Donoghue greeted him, walked by with her usual self-conscious, feminine walk through the swing-doors, and left Patel to speak to Carmichael.

"We're nearly at the end of the list, so Kalinsky can go down to X-ray and then come up for his plaster. He won't need an anaesthetic this time."

"I know that," said Carmichael coldly. "He wouldn't have had any lunch if he had been going to have an anaesthetic."

"Of course, Sister, of course. I'm sorry."

Carmichael turned on her heel and walked into the ward with Patel. They approached the boy, and Dr. Patel went on: "We'll do that in about"—he looked at his watch—"oh, somewhere about three-thirty, I should think. We'll have to go on until then. There's the knee yet, isn't there?"

"Yes, and you've got to finish the shoulder, or is it done?"

"Oh yes, that's how I got out. It'll be down in a minute," said Patel. "I'm going back to have some coffee, then I'll be seeing you, young man."

"All right, Paki. I hope there's an Englishman up there to see fair play," said Leo Kalinsky. He was still sitting on the side of the bed, thumbing through a magazine.

Patel looked at him, dislike in his eyes, but said nothing. He turned back to Carmichael and they went out of the ward, Patel making a heavy, clumping noise in his theatre boots.

CHAPTER 18

Dr. Patel was obviously rather anxious to leave the ward, but, as Carmichael suspected that he'd only come down to get a quick gossip with Minter, she did not let him go when he asked:

"Is there anything else you want me for, Sister?"

"Yes, there is. I'm a bit worried about old Mrs. Bradshaw—you know, the one who had her hip pinned five days ago. She's getting very confused and noisy and I'm afraid, as you know they often do, she may get worse in the night and disturb people."

"Do you mean you want to get her transferred before she gets too bad? If so, there's nothing I can do at the moment, Sister. The geriatric bed situation is awful—I'm sure you know that—and it seems to get worse, not better."

"I know, but I'm just warning you. If she keeps disturbing the ward, I can't keep her. I'm not having the rest of the patients kept awake all night because she's making such a row. She is calling out during the daytime now, but up to the moment the nights haven't been too bad."

"Do you want me to increase her sedation?" asked Patel.

Carmichael went to the note tray and took out Mrs. Bradshaw's notes, took them into her office and placed them on her desk, Patel reluctantly following her.

"Please," she said. "She wants something stronger than she's on now, if not tonight, then tomorrow night. I think she's going to be a bit of a trial—"

Patel cut her off with some irritation, "Well, give me the notes, Sister," and sat down and wrote hastily on the drug sheet and left the office saying, "I must get back. They'll be wondering where I am." He went through the swing-doors and Carmichael heard him climbing the stairs back to the operating theatre.

At six o'clock Carmichael was due to go off, but delays on an operating day made her slightly later and it was five to seven before she was able to leave the ward in charge of Staff Nurse Minter.

"I've reported to Miss O'Donoghue about those two visitors of Leo Kalinsky's, and if they come you'll have to do what you can, but try to discipline them. You'll have to be hard, and don't let them come into my office. Close the door if necessary."

"I'll do my best, Sister. This is a new thing isn't it? Here, I mean. Yobbos coming in and doing what they like. I wouldn't trust them. When they threaten things—you know, like they did with you with that extension—I believe they would cut it. I think they'd drag a drip out of an arm or anything."

"Oh, come along, Staff Nurse, you're exaggerating. They're just, what is it—all mouth and no substance. I wouldn't take too much notice. Just be firm with them." Carmichael opened the drawer and took out her handbag. "I must go now. Anyway, I'm nearly an hour late off as it is."

"All right, Sister, I'll do my best."

Carmichael left the ward. As she went by the lift she automatically glanced at the doors and saw one was slightly ajar. Tentatively she pulled the handle and the door opened slightly. She pulled, but the door would not open completely. If it did, that would be very dangerous, she thought. If anyone thought the lift was there and the door opened and they stepped . . . Good Lord! Why didn't the administration do something about it? The inefficiency was appalling. She pushed the lift door hard and it clicked shut, and then she walked down the stairs.

She checked that the lift doors were properly closed on the next floor. They appeared to be completely shut, and there was no lift there, either, just a black space behind the round glass windows in the wooden doors.

On the ground floor she had another look. There was the lift. She opened the doors and saw that the grille was not properly shut. She pulled it back a little and slammed it to, then closed the outer doors. As she did so, there was a click and the lift started upwards. Obviously somebody from the theatre or the next floor had been trying to get it and couldn't because of the improperly latched door. Carmichael shook her head. Well, she couldn't take on the problems of the entire hospital. She went on to the changing-room, then out of the front door and got into her car, thinking that when she got a top job in the hospital she would see to it that everything ran smoothly, hospital secretary or not.

She pulled out the choke of her car impatiently, turned it round and drove out of the gate, remembering as she did so that she had ignored the telephonist's "Good night." Oh well, they didn't like her particularly anyway, so it didn't matter.

She drove out of the gate and onto the now-darkening road. October was nearly over, winter lay ahead, but she didn't mind too much. The cats didn't like it, though. She had to get them in earlier out of the rain and cold. But it was so cosy in her cottage with the fire. Oh no, she didn't really mind the winter. She liked the television and cooking herself an evening meal, and, after all, she thought fondly, the cats are wonderful company.

Carmichael drove into her garage, turned off the engine, and came out and pushed the doors to. Almost every time she did this she thought that when she had a little more money she must do something about her garage. Still, she'd done so much to the cottage and she couldn't do it all at once. But the garage was a cover for the car, and the doors had dropped on their hinges and needed attention. She felt she must do something about it before the really bad weather came.

She went along the small path that led up to her front door, got out her key and had almost put it in the lock when she realized the door was already open. Burglars? she wondered. She was frightened for a moment and then wondered if she had forgotten to lock the door that morning. No, she was sure she had locked it securely. She always tried it before she left. She pushed the door open cautiously, switched on the light, and stood there hardly able to believe her eyes.

CHAPTER 19

The little room was wrecked. The small table standing just inside the door was overturned and one leg broken off. The mirror above it was smashed and the wall covered with what looked like blood, but as she smelled it she realized it was tomato sauce. All the furniture had been overturned. The lamp in the corner that she had bought only three weeks ago was lying on its side and the shade had been squashed—stamped on, by the look of it. The walls were sprayed, too, with what looked like aluminium paint. Nearly everything was broken. The mantelpiece was swept clean of all its small ornaments, which lay on the floor, most of them smashed. She went forward automatically, feeling quite numb. She bent down and picked up one of the ornaments. It was still intact, and she put it back on the mantelpiece and then realized what a foolish thing that was to have done.

The television had been kicked in and lay on its side. She turned and went through into the kitchen. It was the same there. Everything seemed to be on the floor. The contents of the cupboards were strewn about everywhere, the drawers hanging open. She trod on rice, flour, and sugar. It was a scene of havoc.

She turned and rushed upstairs and found to her surprise and some relief that there was less damage there. The bed had been stripped and overturned and the bedclothes lay scattered round her bedroom. All the drawers containing her underclothes were open and the contents scattered, but there was nothing smeared on the walls.

She went to her jewel box and opened it—goodness knows, she had little enough jewellery. It was empty. Her perfume,

the perfume that she had gone on buying ever since Harry
... that had gone.

She went down again to the kitchen, went to a small box where she saved twenty-pence pieces ready to pay the gardener or the window cleaner. It was empty.

It was then, like a physical blow, that she thought of the cats, and as she thought of them a pain went through her chest. She felt suddenly as if she couldn't breathe. If they'd ... if they'd hurt her cats ... She opened the back door and called. A fine rain had begun to fall. She called and called and went out into the rain, oblivious of it, looking up to see whether Torty or Tibbles had run up into the trees to hide—they were timid of strangers. She hoped ... Surely they'd run ... Then she remembered that she had shot the bolt on the little cat-door because it had been raining when she left this morning and she had thought they had better stay in and use the cat tray. They didn't like it, but they put up with it, and they were always doubly glad when she got back if they had been left indoors, because then they knew she would let them go out.

Oh, God! Whoever had done all this could have caught them, hurt them, killed them. She closed the back door and looked down at the cat-flap. At the bottom the bolt was drawn back, and more tomato ketchup was on the flap itself, on the bolt. She examined it more closely and she saw that this time it was not tomato ketchup, it was blood.

Carmichael was conscious of a whistling in her ears and a dimming of her vision. She thought she was going to faint. She went into the sitting-room, righted the armchair, and put her head between her knees. After a few seconds the feeling went off and she got up and picked up the phone, which, to her astonishment, was still working, and she dialled the police. They would come, but who had done it? The question was superfluous, she knew who had done it. It was the two she had seen last night on the motor bike, and she had no doubt who they were. They had followed her home from the hospital to see where she lived, seen her put the car away, and then driven on down the lane and come back. It was those two, the girl and the boy, Leo's friends. That's how they had got their own back. That's why Leo had warned her with those hooded eyes of his. He'd looked at her so complacently, so sure of himself.

She gazed round the little room. Years of work, years of thought, decorating, waiting till she could afford to buy the kind of wallpaper she liked—all destroyed. She tentatively touched the aluminium paint. It smeared her fingertip. She looked at it and unconsciously wiped it down the side of her skirt. It might wash off the walls, she thought, but what about the television, what about everything? Most of all, what about the cats? She hardly dared think of Tibbles and Torty. If they had done anything to the cats, she would kill those black riders. Oh yes, if they'd hurt her cats she would kill them, somehow.

She went out of the back door again, still indifferent to the rain, her hair getting wetter and wetter and the water running down her face. She was crying, too, as she called, but there was no answering miaow, no sign of the two cats running towards her as they always did, their tails erect. Nothing. Just the darkening garden and the rain. She went back into the cottage, but she couldn't stay there, and when the police at last arrived they had difficulty in making anyone hear because she was out again in the orchard, wandering round the trees, still calling. She came back into the cottage to be greeted by two tall policemen standing in the front doorway. They followed her into the sitting-room.

"Oh, Lord!" said the younger policeman. "What a mess, miss, what a mess. Do you know who did it?"

"I'm not sure. Two people on a motor bike followed me home last night. Then I saw them go up the lane, and they obviously must have turned round because they went by again going in the other direction as I came in."

"Would you recognize them if you saw them again?"

"No. They had helmets on and those things over their faces, the black glass. No, no, I wouldn't."

"Well, we'll have to take fingerprints. It might be someone we know. Anything missing?"

"My cats, both of them," said Carmichael, and again felt this dizzy feeling come over her. She sat down abruptly.

Another car drew up outside, a plain clothes policeman followed by a policewoman in uniform came up the path. The policewoman, a pretty girl, came straight in and put her arm round Carmichael.

"Why, you're soaked through. Can I get you a towel?" She looked round. "It's horrible, horrible. Is there anywhere you can go, anywhere you could stay? Relatives perhaps?"

Carmichael shook her head. "I can't. I can't leave, because my cats Tibbles and Torty might come back. They may be hurt. They may have tortured them."

The policewoman nodded understandingly. "I see. Well, there're a couple of cottages just down the road, aren't there? Mrs. . . ." She looked up at the young policeman. "You know, she recently lost her husband . . . Mrs. Sampson."

"I can't stay with her," said Carmichael. "I can't bother her, if you don't mind. I'll stay here and lock the door up somehow."

"Well, I suppose they won't come back, but what have they taken?"

"I told you, my cats," said Carmichael irritably.

"Yes, I know, but what valuables?" asked the older policeman.

"Valuables!" Carmichael almost spat it out. "My cats, they're the valuables, there's nothing else that matters but them."

The policeman's eyes met those of the woman constable's and a look passed between them that Carmichael could not understand.

"Well, I was meaning for insurance, you know. You're insured?"

"Yes, of course. Of course I'm insured."

"Well, that will cover the damage," said the policeman almost lamely. "And now we'll have a look round, if we may."

"Of course you may."

There were four policemen now, but it didn't matter, they couldn't do anything.

Then the policewoman spoke softly: "Perhaps your cats are hiding under a bed or inside a cupboard. Have you looked?"

Carmichael looked at her with sudden hope, a sudden liking. "No, I haven't. I've only been outside. I thought they'd . . ."

"Well, come on, then, let's look!" said the policewoman, and together they went round the small cottage, looking in the cupboard, under the spare-room bed and in the kitchen units.

The girl was sympathetic—she herself was a cat lover, she said—but there was no Torty and no Tibbles nor any sign of them.

"If you don't mind, I'll go outside again," said Carmichael. She knew that her hair was rain-soaked from when she was out before, but it didn't matter.

Carmichael left the police looking for signs that would give some indication about who could have broken in, to find clues to something Carmichael already knew. What could they do if they caught them? Fine them twenty-five pounds, perhaps? Slap their wrists as that man Maynard had said, something like that. She had heard of what happened in these cases, she'd seen it in the papers. She wouldn't tell them who had done it. No, she would settle with them herself.

Out in the orchard she stood for a moment leaning against a tree, quietly, before she started calling again. She would be up all night, she knew. She suddenly decided that she could do more than this and went back into the cottage and got her torch and started walking round the hedge surrounding the garden, looking underneath to see if one of them had crawled there to die or had been thrown there, flashing the torch to and fro over the uneven grass, looking for blood tracks to see if either of them had tried to get away. Her eyes followed the movement of the light from side to side, but there was nothing.

She looked back at her little cottage. All the lights were on upstairs and down and she could see the police passing the lighted windows, searching, looking. She suddenly put out her torch, stopped calling, and went into a far corner of the garden. It was very dark, where the beams of light from the windows did not reach, and she was violently sick.

CHAPTER 20

Carmichael came in from the garden and found that the police were almost ready to leave. The two uniformed men looked tired, the other two less so. Carmichael offered them a cup of tea and they gratefully accepted. She made it still feeling a terrible nausea. She must have looked pale and red-eyed, for one of the policemen said:

"You'll get over it, miss. It's a terrible shock at first. Everybody feels the same. It's having your things all looked through and touched, you know, awful. Better have your lock replaced fairly quickly."

Carmichael looked at him vacantly, and it was a second or two before she answered. "Yes, I will, and thank you. Did you —did you notice the blood on the cat-flap?" She had wanted to ask this question the whole time they had been there and yet had not dared to do so. The reply heartened her.

"Yes, yes we did, Miss Carmichael. We've taken a sample of it. One of them probably cut his hand. Was the cat-door fastened when you left this morning?"

"Yes, I bolted it, that little bolt at the bottom, do you see?" Carmichael bent down and touched the door. "I wanted to keep the cats in because it was raining. I didn't want them to get wet without me here to dry them. They've got a litter tray." She added the explanation but felt it was unnecessary, for the policeman smiled broadly.

"Well then, someone must have unbolted it and the blood got on it then. It's on the bolt even. Could be from a cut finger."

"Or they have hurt my cats." Carmichael's voice quivered,

and again the policewoman's eyes narrowed in sympathy, but the policeman replied:

"Oh, I don't know, miss. The intruder could have cut his hand smashing the television. We shall be able to tell you whether it's human or animal blood."

"Will you let me know straight away, as soon as you know, I mean? That's the most important thing," said Carmichael, and the other policeman said quickly:

"Yes, of course we will, miss. Don't worry. I bet the cats are all right. My wife's got three and they dash out if there's anything like this going on. They go off and hide for a bit. They're not foolish, cats, they wouldn't stay around even like a dog would. They'd clear out."

"But they couldn't get out," said Carmichael, looking at him grateful nevertheless.

"Well, perhaps they let them out. You never know what these yobbos will do. They might have liked cats."

These were the best words of cheer that Carmichael had had, and yet when she thought of that girl and boy visiting the ward, she wondered.

In the kitchen, after the plain clothes man had come down from upstairs and joined the others for a cup of tea, they stood there silently drinking, and then they all departed, the three uniformed police in the police car and the detective in an ordinary car.

It was completely dark now, and Carmichael felt very vulnerable for the moment. She looked at the broken lock of the front door and wondered how she could secure it. She closed it and then got a chair and wedged it under the handle. It was fairly secure, and anyway she wouldn't be going to bed tonight. She'd be up all night looking for Torty and Tibbles.

Minutes after the police had gone away, she was out again in the back garden calling, but no cat came. She was beginning to despair and was frightened of the feeling, as it seemed similar to the one she had felt in the psychiatric ward. She wondered if all this would put her back there. She re-entered the cottage and decided that she'd spend the night clearing up, then ring the hospital in the morning and tell them that she wouldn't be in. Once daylight came, the search for the cats could continue if they hadn't come back during the night.

Carmichael scrubbed the walls and got the tomato ketchup off. There was little staining. It was a laborious task and took her hours, but she didn't mind. Every time she stopped for a little rest, out into the garden she went calling, then came back and got on with the work.

She felt a strange reluctance to put her underclothes back into the drawers and her other clothes into the wardrobe when she went up into the bedroom. She snatched all the lining paper out of the drawers and put in fresh. She had a longing to wash everything but dismissed it as foolish. She couldn't do that now.

The rain continued falling softly outside as she worked. She wiped out the wardrobe with disinfectant and hung up her clothes again and packed things back into the freshly lined drawers.

When the cottage began to assume something of its normal appearance, she felt slightly better. Downstairs in the sitting-room she found the aluminium paint was impossible to remove. She would have to paper over it. Luckily she still had several rolls of the paper, and there would be enough. She would do that when she felt stronger, when she had recovered and the cats had come back.

She looked ruefully at the television. It was upright now and she had swept up the scattered glass, looking carefully at the fragments to see if there was blood on them. She found none, but she still hoped that the policeman was right and that somehow either the girl or the boy had cut themselves. She was positive who it was who had done all this, but she didn't want to think about it too much. When she met them again she would deal with them.

She had emptied the debris into the dustbin outside and stood for ten minutes in the rain calling. She looked at her watch. The clock in the sitting-room had been knocked off the mantelpiece onto the floor, and it had stopped. The policeman had noted the time, thinking it might be then, seven o'clock, when they had come, although he couldn't be sure that the clock had stopped at the moment of impact. They had been good, the police, and she had appreciated it. They had been kind—especially the policewoman.

Carmichael suddenly felt incredibly tired. It was three-thirty a.m. She went and poured herself a large glass of sherry and sat drinking it on the chair in the kitchen with the back door wide open so that she could see into the garden. The rain still fell, a soft rain that would do the garden good, but if the cats were lying anywhere injured, this could kill them. She shivered and got up. She couldn't bear to close the back door, though the cat-flap was swinging free.

After the sherry she went into the sitting-room, switched on her electric fire and sat by it for the rest of the night, waiting for the two wet frightened cats to come in. Every noise that the trees made outside made her think it was them and she got up each time and went and looked out, but there was only the rain and the darkness.

At about five-thirty she must have sunk into an exhausted sleep because suddenly when she looked at her watch again it was seven-fifteen and daylight. She was thankful for this and made herself tea, shivering with cold, the back door still open. At last she shut it, thinking that if they came she would hear them. If only . . . if only . . . She gazed at the flap. If only a small head would poke through . . . She finished her tea and looked round the cottage. There was still a lot to be done, but she felt she couldn't do any more at the moment. She just sat down and apathetically gazed at the broken television.

At eight o'clock she rang the hospital, told the telephonist what had happened, and asked her to convey the message to Miss O'Donoghue when she came in. The telephonist tried to be sympathetic, but Carmichael cut her off. She didn't wish to speak to anybody. Certainly she didn't wish to speak to her Nursing Officer. She felt she would cry and make a fool of herself. Perhaps Miss O'Donoghue wouldn't understand about the cats. Of course she'd be shocked about the vandalism, and she would understand Carmichael's taking the day off—that was no worry.

Carmichael was surprised when a ray of sunshine came through the kitchen window and played on the water in which she had started washing up her glass and cup and saucer. Somehow it seemed a better omen. She would find them. It would be warmer now and the rain had stopped. It would be better. She would go out now and widen her search, going round the adjoining field and even down as far as the cottages along the road where Mrs. Sampson lived. She stopped. She'd entirely forgotten about Jack Sampson—the cats had filled every scrap of her horizon.

Later she looked in the yellow pages of her telephone directory and rang a locksmith. She told him the situation and he said he'd come straight out and put on a new lock. Within half an hour he had arrived. When he saw the state of the sitting-room, the paint, and the television, he whistled.

"One of those do's, eh? Yes, we've had one or two in the town. It's disgusting. Can't see what they get out of it. And what punishment do they get? Not much, not nearly enough."

Carmichael told him about the cats, and again his reply, like the policeman's, was reassuring:

"They'll come back. Cats always run away and hide if they're frightened. Don't worry. I expect they're huddled somewhere, you know, waiting to see if it's all clear."

"It's a long time and there was blood on the cat-door." Carmichael took him through to the kitchen and pointed.

"Well, that's not so good. Might have been hurt, mightn't they? You don't know what they'll get up to, some vandals. They'll get hold of a—"

"Please don't tell me." Carmichael stopped him and he nodded understandingly.

"Right, let's get on then," he said and went and examined the front door again. He looked at the splinters round the lock. "I can cover this. I'll put a mortise on, a big one. They suit these cottages. You'll have to have a bigger key. Luckily I brought one with me."

"Do just as you think," said Carmichael, and he proceeded to whistle cheerfully as he worked, and Carmichael, almost ashamed now to do any more calling, left him to it and went out into the garden to start searching again silently.

When she came back into the cottage at about ten o'clock, the locksmith had finished. He told her how much she owed him and she fetched her handbag.

"Don't you worry, miss, that'll keep anybody out. Is the back door all right? They didn't touch that, did they?"

"No. No, it's all right, thank you."

As Carmichael handed him the money she noticed that her hand was sweating. The key he handed her was, as he had said, bigger than her last one, and somehow it was reassuring. As he turned to leave he said to her kindly:

"Now, don't worry, they'll be back, them cats."

Carmichael walked to the front gate with him and he closed it carefully, then got into his van, turning round to say "Cheerio."

"Cheerio," said Carmichael and thought it was the most inappropriate good-bye she had ever said.

CHAPTER 21

Carmichael made herself coffee. She'd got to keep going, she told herself, she'd got to find them, and if she had nothing to eat or drink that wouldn't help. It was going to be a terrible day. She was interrupted just as she was making the coffee by a knock on the front door. She put down the cup and saucer and hurried to open it, turning the big key. There on the doorstep stood Jack Sampson's wife, Helen.

"I heard what happened, Sister Carmichael. My neighbour Doris told me, and we wondered if you was all right. You don't look much, but who would? That's awful."

"It's very, very good of you to come. Yes, I'm all right, and you?"

Helen Sampson shrugged. "Getting over it, I guess. I'll feel better after the funeral . . . They say you do, don't they?"

The two women faced each other in the doorway of the little cottage. Carmichael's mind was in a turmoil. She felt strangely above the scene as if she was looking down on it. She had killed this woman's husband, and now she had come, a bereaved wife, to give some kind of solace to her. Instead of guilt, however, she felt a kinship with the woman. She remembered Sampson's blood running down the side of the road in the rain. She was silent for such a long time that Mrs. Sampson said:

"I'll go away. I shouldn't 'ave come. I only thought . . ."

"Oh, I'm sorry, please come in. I felt . . . I haven't got . . . You know what I mean."

"Yes, I do know what you mean. It's sort of up in the air, isn't it? You can't really feel it's true when something horrible happens."

"It's the cats, that's the worst part. They've disappeared and

I don't know . . . There was blood on the cat-door and I can't help wondering if it's theirs, if they've done something . . . The police have taken a sample, but I don't know what to think."

Quite suddenly Carmichael, to her own disgust and embarrassment, began to sob and Mrs. Sampson's eyes immediately filled with tears as well. Carmichael turned away and felt the woman's hand almost timidly touch her shoulder. She tried to pull herself together. She always hated showing her feelings in front of other people.

"I'll make us some coffee," she said and Helen Sampson came a little farther into the sitting-room.

"Do sit down, do sit down," Carmichael said, and Helen Sampson went across and sat on the edge of a chair, looking round her.

Carmichael went into the kitchen. When she came back into the sitting-room carrying the cups, Mrs. Sampson held something out to her.

"Look," she said, "this was there under the television. I picked it up. It's part of the screen, isn't it?" She held it gingerly between her thumb and forefinger. "There's blood on it, look." She pointed and Carmichael took the piece of jagged glass in her hand and saw a smear of dull red in the corner.

"Looks like they cut themselves, did themselves some kind of injury. They probably let the cats out to get them out of the way, that's how the blood got on the flap."

Carmichael sat down heavily in the chair opposite Helen Sampson. It seemed as though a ray of light had come into the room.

"Thank you, Mrs. Sampson, I can never thank you enough for finding that."

She laid the piece of glass carefully on the coffee-table beside her, then handed Mrs. Sampson her cup of coffee.

"I only found a bit of glass, Sister Carmichael." Helen Sampson looked slightly surprised. "That's so awful . . . I've got a cat and I know. They've run away, I expect. They were frightened and they ran away—all that crashing about—that's what cats do. Mine was away for two days once. Nearly drove me wild, it did. We're fond of her—I mean, I am."

"That's what everybody says, but they didn't come back last night. It was raining and they don't like rain. I always dry them when they get wet. I was half the night calling, but it was no good. Perhaps they . . ." A new thought had struck her. Perhaps they had been cut from the glass of the television, walked on it, perhaps. "Today I'm going to look all round the field and everywhere."

"I'll help you. You go one way and I'll go the other. After all, we can cover more ground if we're both looking, can't we? They won't come to me, perhaps, but I can tell you if I see them."

Carmichael looked at her mutely, then she said, "You must miss your husband. That must be dreadful."

Helen Sampson looked at her levelly for a moment, then dropped her eyes. "I shall miss him, yes. But, Sister, he wasn't a good man, you know, not to me, I mean. He drank too much and he had these girls, nurses, sometimes, I'm afraid to say. Then there were the cleaners. He brought one home once, thought I was out. Well, I was. I'd gone to my sister's but I got back sooner than he thought. I wasn't happy with him. I suppose I'm sorry he died like that, but they say he didn't know much about it and there it is. Mrs. Pilcher—you know, Doris, my next door neighbour, the one who you saw in the car—she's been ever so good to me and she says she wouldn't have stood it for a day, not the way he went on. He knocked me about. He wasn't a nice man. They say don't speak ill of the dead, but I don't believe in that. What was, was, and it can't change. I guess he's answering for it now he's dead, eh? I dunno. I'll be glad when he's buried. You know, I wouldn't have wished him dead, but I can't grieve all that much. Do you think it's wrong?"

The two women sat looking at each other. Carmichael suddenly thought of Jones's mother way back, and how she, Carmichael, had got rid of the old woman. A husband was different, perhaps, but maybe it was rather like Jones. Jack Sampson wasn't really loved. Then again, he wasn't really like that beastly old woman. Still, he was better dead. For the first time since she had discovered the break-in, Carmichael gave a wintry smile and Mrs. Sampson smiled back, drained her coffee-cup, and said:

"The silver paint on the walls, I'll help you with that too, if you like, when we've found the cats." Carmichael looked at her and nodded. "Well, come on, Sister, let's start. We've got to find those pussy-cats, dead or alive."

Carmichael shuddered, but she knew what Helen Sampson meant. At least, if they found them dead, they would know that they weren't suffering anywhere, half dead.

"Yes, we must get on," she said, picking up the coffee-cups and taking them into the kitchen. "We must find them, as you say, dead or alive, but, oh, how I hope, alive."

Helen Sampson followed Carmichael out into the kitchen and said something that momentarily threw Carmichael off balance:

"Will you be coming to the funeral? I mean, you knew him."

Carmichael stopped, her back to Mrs. Sampson, and didn't speak for quite a few seconds, then she answered abruptly:

"Yes. Well, I don't know. Someone will represent the Sisters." She turned and faced the woman behind her. "I did know him, as you say, but we'll have to see."

The same wintry smile as Carmichael's came over Mrs. Sampson's face. "Yes. Perhaps I shouldn't have said the things I did. When it's all over and things are settled, perhaps you'd come and see me," she said.

It was a friendly remark and Carmichael recognized it as such, but felt repelled at the idea of going into Sampson's cottage.

"Perhaps," she said. Her voice was not superior, and Mrs. Sampson obviously accepted it for what it was, a half refusal, but was not offended, and they parted to start the search. Carmichael noticed that Helen Sampson limped a little and she remembered her cold remark to the porter about his wife's knee and the operating list.

They continued walking and calling, getting farther and farther apart, and then eventually they met at the far end of the garden, but they had found nothing. At last Helen Sampson decided she must leave, and Carmichael watched her go up the garden path, out of the gate and down the lane, turning to wave her hand as she did so. In a way, she was sorry to see her go. She had never felt so close to anyone before, in such a strange way. She realized, of course, that it was their mutual search that had done this. It had done nothing to relieve her misery, but at least it had been offered help, someone to talk to.

She watched her disappear out of sight down the lane, then she turned back into the house. She felt she couldn't stop looking or calling. Again she felt this faintness and dizziness and realized she had not eaten for goodness knows how long.

Tomorrow she must go back to the hospital and leave the cottage empty, the cat-door of course unbolted. She could only pray that when she came back . . . She almost started to follow Mrs. Sampson, to call after her, to ask her if she would come back during the day tomorrow to see if the cats were there and feed them, but she felt, although she couldn't explain it, that to do so would be "bad luck." Perhaps it was that she did not want to link up the death of Jack Sampson and her cats. She was not sure.

CHAPTER 22

The next morning Carmichael left the cottage with reluctance to go back to work. She almost wished again that she had asked Mrs. Sampson to look in to see if the cats had returned, but the woman's presence reminded her too much of the macabre scene she wanted to get out of her mind.

Today she was on duty until five. In a way this was good. It meant it would still be light when she came home to search for the cats if they had not returned, and if they had not, they might do so in the quiet of the evening. Her thoughts swayed to and fro as she drove to the hospital. She narrowly missed going over a red light, a thing that Carmichael, a meticulous driver, would normally never do. She began to worry again about her own mind. She had felt so like this when Margaret Tarrant had appeared on the scene that terrible day when she had been with Harry. No, she mustn't think herself into a depression that would put her in a psychiatric ward, making her lose her job. She must hang on to her sanity, not doubt the integrity of her own mind.

As she drove into her parking-place at the hospital, she felt a sudden uplift, a feeling that the cats would come back. One moment she felt one way, the next another. She didn't like this swinging of her emotions, the feeling of optimism so closely followed by pessimism. It was unsettling, unnatural.

She got out of her car and stood for a moment with her hands on the top of the mini thinking, gazing at the front of the hospital without seeing it. She locked the car, walked over, and realized, when she got to the door, that she had left her handbag in the car and went back.

She glanced at her watch—ten minutes late and she'd still

got to change. She hurried up to the changing-room, got into her uniform, and went to her ward.

"I'm late, Nurse Minter," she said. "I was held up on the road. I thought I'd never get here." Her voice gave nothing away, nothing of the tension inside her, and her Staff Nurse answered with tremendous sympathy:

"How awful for you—I mean, yesterday. I'm so sorry. Miss O'Donoghue told us what had happened to your cottage. Aren't they the end. I had a friend . . . they bashed her doors down, there was no need for it, they could have just broken the locks, some of the doors weren't even locked, but they hacked them down with a chopper. It was terrible. What did the police do? Were they helpful? I don't know how you can come to work. I think you're very brave."

Carmichael turned her white face towards her. "It's the cats," she said, and then wished she hadn't, for she suddenly burst into tears. Minter looked embarrassed and awkwardly put an arm round her shoulders and drew her into the office.

Carmichael sat down and took out some tissues from the drawer, blotted her eyes angrily, and tried to resume her Sister's voice: "I'm sorry, Staff Nurse, I didn't mean to, it's just . . . it's the cats you see, there was blood on the cat-door. I'm terribly worried."

Minter held her shoulder a little more tightly. "They've probably run away. Cats do, you know. We had one that stayed away for three weeks and then came back. She was thin but she was all right. Something must have frightened her. She never did it again."

Everyone seemed to have a cat that had run away, or said they had. Carmichael doubted whether it was the truth, but it was said to comfort her. By this time she had partially regained her composure.

"All right, Staff Nurse," she said briskly, "please tell me what night nurse said. She's gone, I presume."

"Yes, I hope you don't mind, but we hardly expected you. I explained to her that you might not come in. I've taken the report." Minter proceeded to go through the patients with

Carmichael and this helped, although she could not put her mind entirely on what her Staff Nurse was saying. She forced herself to listen and it helped.

". . . and old Mrs. Bradshaw, she's been terribly noisy. I asked Mr. Dalby yesterday if he could do anything about it but—"

"You shouldn't have done that, it's nothing to do with him. It's the house officer's problem to get rid of obstreperous patients like that and it's got to be done. I must get Dr. Patel or Dr. Manning. I'll ring, well, in half an hour. I'll tell them it's imperative."

At that moment a yell came from the women's ward, quickly followed by the soothing voice of a nurse, but the shouting persisted.

"That's her," said Staff Nurse Minter. "She's had plenty of sedatives and she's only slept for about two hours. They were fed up, Sister, and the patients are too. I'd be glad if you could get hold of one of the doctors and perhaps you could tell the night nurse that she's going to be moved. Poor old girl, she can't help it, but it does disturb the others."

"Did you see him yesterday? Patel, I mean? It's no use talking to a Consultant Staff Nurse." Her voice was again reproachful. "You can't approach the Consultant with trivial things like that."

"I know, Sister, but I did ask Dr. Manning. We rang him and asked him to come up and write up some extra sedatives for her. That was when she was climbing over the cot side. She really is . . . Well, you know . . ."

"I know only too well. I'll get hold of him and she must be moved. She can't stay in an acute ward like mine."

Carmichael was resuming so much of her old manner that her Staff Nurse looked relieved. Carmichael's crying had really been a bit unnerving. She'd never seen Carmichael relax or give way to any feeling, no matter what happened, except perhaps rage when something went wrong on the ward. The whole time she had been on the orthopaedic wards, or for that matter the few times she had met her when she was in Casualty, she'd always been cold and usually unruffled, though there was a rumour that she had been in a psychiatric hospital.

"That's all then, Sister," said Staff Nurse Minter. "Oh, I forgot, those awful people didn't come yesterday. Leo was a bit miffed. He's been smoking again out of hours. Burnt his sheet, too. I gave him a right rollicking. He won't get up. He's supposed to. He may be going home tomorrow, or so Mr. Dalby said yesterday. I wish he'd said he could go home straight away, but he didn't. Anyway, he's got an appointment for the fracture clinic next week, so if he does go home tomorrow, Sister, that's that. I'll be glad to see the back of him."

Carmichael nodded. The very thought of Leo Kalinsky's friends brought back the scene at the cottage.

"They'll both come today, I suppose."

"I suppose so, although they may not. They didn't yesterday, or, come to that, did they come the day before? I don't believe they did. Surely I would have remembered," she said ruefully.

Carmichael remembered. "Yes, I think they did. They have a motor bike, haven't they?" she asked.

"I don't know. I suppose so. They look as if they have one—not that you can always tell, and I've never seen them in helmets."

"I think they have," said Carmichael reflectively, then, "We must get on, Staff Nurse. I'll do my round."

The women's ward was quiet for the moment as Carmichael went in. Each patient she visited, however, was swift to complain about Mrs. Bradshaw's noise.

"We've 'ad a night, I can tell you, Sister. It's too bad, really it is. She kept on all the time and she does it in the day, too. She threw her dinner at Nurse yesterday—that one." She pointed to a nurse who was busy remaking the bottom of a bed on the other side of the ward, having just done a dressing on the patient's foot. "Threw the dinner at that one, covered her with it. She was going to feed her, you see, and she suddenly took the plate and slammed it at her. I know she can't help it, but she shouldn't be here, should she, Sister?"

Carmichael shook her head and proceeded to the next bed to receive a similar tirade. One patient like Mrs. Bradshaw in a ward like this could ruin the nights and days.

She got to the last patient, a young girl, pretty, wearing a diaphanous night-dress, her red hair curled round her head. She looked at Carmichael and grinned.

"She's a bit of an old devil, isn't she? I know she can't help it. My gran went like that. Dreadful, it was. She trundled off down the street in her night-dress once. The police brought her back. We didn't know she'd gone, we were looking at telly. They bundled her off to the psychiatric ward. She soon died, though. Well, it was better, really. After all, she wasn't any good to herself, if you know what I mean."

"Yes, I do," said Carmichael and walked out of the ward knowing that the girl's eyes were following her curiously. She felt that her women patients could never quite make her out. Perhaps they didn't like her, but then she thought they didn't dislike her. The men patients were usually rather scared of her, except Leo Kalinsky. She supposed reluctantly that she'd have to do a round in the men's ward now and see that young man.

CHAPTER 23

In the men's ward, contrary to what Minter had said, Leo was not in his bed but was sitting in an armchair in the middle of the ward looking at a comic, which he held in one hand half-supported by the other. He looked up as Carmichael came up to him, a curious expression on his face.

"Hallo, Sis, been off sick then? Didn't see you yesterday. Nurse said you were ill, it wasn't your day off," he said.

Their eyes met and Carmichael realized in a second that he knew, he knew everything that had happened. A slight smile twisted his face. She would have liked to hit him. The telephone, she thought, they probably phoned him, as they hadn't visited, to tell him, to gloat. She was almost on the point of asking him if he had had a telephone call from his friends, but she merely said coldly:

"Yes, I had a little domestic trouble. Thank you for noticing that I was off duty."

It was sarcasm and he recognized it immediately and his grin widened. "Oh, what is it they say? Absence makes the heart grow fonder, Sister? I may be going home today. You'll be glad to get rid of me. Got to come back, though, to that poxy fracture clinic. My mum had to come when she broke her wrist before she went off. They kept her waiting three hours. S'pose I'll have to wait about the same time?"

"Well, you've hardly got anything else to do, have you? You can't drive a motor bike, not with that arm."

The boy looked up quickly. "Drive a motor bike? I can't afford a bloody motor bike. I'm unemployed, remember? Wish I could, though. I'd have one soon enough."

"Like your friend Douglas?"

"Yeah, though his isn't very big. 'E can't afford . . . You can pay about four thousand pounds, yer know, if you want something really flash, and that's what I want."

It was enough. Carmichael had just wanted assurance that they did have a motor bike, those two.

She went round the rest of the men's ward, speaking quietly to each patient. Usually she preferred the men's ward to the women's. The few things the men did, like not keeping their lockers tidy or not keeping quiet as they should when Mr. Dalby was doing a round, these things she found not so bad as the whining some women did. An old man stopped her as she was just about to go out of the ward. She was passing his bed when he called.

She went up close to him. "Is it true what I heard, that your cottage was wrecked?"

"Yes. How did you know about it?"

"As a matter of fact, *he* told me." He pointed to the chair where Leo was sitting. "He said it had been . . . I forget what he said, but I think he meant vandalized. I am sorry. You spoke to me about your place before and how nice you'd got it, remember?"

Yes, she did remember. She had one morning talked quite a bit to this old man, Mr. Birchall, a nice, clean, presentable old man who reminded her a little of what Harry would be like when he got older.

"Leo Kalinsky told you? Thank you, Mr. Birchall. How is your leg feeling?"

"Up and down, Sister. I don't know when I'll get home, do you? They've said they've got to take two more toes off. Do you think that's right?"

Carmichael laid her hand gently on the old man's arm. "It may be, but don't worry."

Mr. Birchall had been transferred from the medical ward with gangrene of the toes. He was diabetic and Carmichael thought it would probably be the foot that would have to come off, not just the toes. She said no more to him, thinking again of Harry and his diabetes and how . . . She stopped her mind going in that direction, patted the old man's arm, turned round and walked back to where Leo Kalinsky was sitting.

"Did you tell Mr. Birchall that my cottage had been vandalized?" she said abruptly. He looked at her tentatively and then said:

"No-o. Did I? Might have, but I don't think so."

"Well, if you did, how did you know?" Her voice was so cold and so menacing that the boy looked startled, almost afraid.

"One of the nurses must have told me, I suppose. I dunno. P'raps the Staff Nurse, or was it that other lady with the blue dress, what's her name, the Irish one?"

"I doubt if anyone would talk about my affairs, but she may have," said Carmichael, and she walked out of the ward to be met almost at once by Miss O'Donoghue, so the chance to ask her was there quicker than she thought. Without a preliminary good morning she said:

"Did you tell Leo Kalinsky the reason I was away yesterday?"

The Nursing Officer looked surprised and a little affronted. "Of course not. I wouldn't discuss a thing like that with a patient, you know that, Carmichael. Whatever makes you ask me such a thing? Neither would any of the other nurses, I'm sure."

Staff Nurse Minter, who was passing, heard what she said, and Carmichael put out a hand to stop her.

"No, Sister, I certainly didn't tell him, and I can't think any of the other nurses would. I did mention it to one or two of them, but they wouldn't have told a patient. I told them they weren't to say anything anyway, and I don't think they did."

"Ask them," said Carmichael abruptly, and Minter nodded vigorously.

"I will, most certainly," she said. It was obvious the Staff Nurse thought that if there had been a leak it must have been through her. She hurried back into the women's ward, where one or two of the nurses were serving morning drinks, the orderly being off sick.

"No, they wouldn't do that," said Miss O'Donoghue. "How do you feel? It was a beastly thing to happen. Of course you had to take the day off. You could have taken today off too. I told Miss Scott, and she sympathizes tremendously and said she'd like to see you this morning. She was quite upset about it."

"Thank you. I'll go and see her at . . . ?"

"Eleven," said Miss O'Donoghue. "She said would you pop into her office at eleven and she'd have a word with you. I had to tell her, of course."

"Of course," said Carmichael, and the two women went into her office, where Carmichael gave Miss O'Donoghue the outline of what Nurse Minter had told her. She spoke about the noisy patient in the women's ward.

"Well, I'll leave you to cope with Patel or Manning. If you can't get them to move her, I'll have a go," said Miss O'Donoghue. "I must go now. I'm late this morning."

"I was late too. I slept badly—as a matter of fact, I didn't sleep at all."

Miss O'Donoghue put her hand on Carmichael's—an unusual gesture. Carmichael did not encourage such things. She prayed that Miss O'Donoghue did not know or would not ask about the cats, that she would not tell her of a case she knew about a cat that had been gone for God knows how long. She didn't, and she merely increased the pressure of her hand on Carmichael's and then left the ward.

Carmichael stood for a second or two trying to wrench her mind back to the ward and to what she had to do next. She was conscious of feeling sick again. It was probably because she had eaten so little, or perhaps it was from anxiety. Then she went over to the ward phone and dialled Dr. Manning, then dialled for some coffee for herself. She felt in need of it. Suddenly, uncharacteristically, she longed for a huge glass of sherry.

Dr. Manning arrived.

"What's wrong? Did you want me?"

Carmichael put her problem to him as forcibly as she could.

"I know, I know about her," he said. "I heard all about it from Patel and I've rung round everywhere. We've tried, Sister, but it's not easy. You know what the geriatric bed situation is like. I promise you I'll do my best."

He did a quick round on both wards and disappeared, and Carmichael wondered if he would be able to do anything about Mrs. Bradshaw. It was unlikely.

In the afternoon the visitors began to arrive promptly and Carmichael sat in the office. She watched carefully for a sign of those two black-clad figures. She didn't know quite why she was waiting for them. She could do nothing, she had no proof, but she just wanted to see them so that she could plan what to do about them, because she knew official channels would do little as usual even if it was proved that they were responsible. What would the sentence be? What would they do to these young hooligans? Not enough.

It was nearly at the end of visiting time that they arrived. They walked through the swing-doors, the girl rubbing her knee. Staff Nurse Minter was just walking out of the ward and passed them.

"That bloody lift of yours didn't come right up to the floor. It stopped and we had to force the bloody doors open to get out. Why don't you have efficient things in hospital? You're supposed to have, you take enough of our money to get them."

"Your money . . . I bet you don't pay anything," said Minter and walked by.

"Shit her, thinks she's everybody just because she's got a uniform on," the girl said as they went by Carmichael's office, and both of them turned and looked at Carmichael, the girl's vermilion lips parting in a smile—or was it a sneer?

"Afternoon, Sister. Our mate's coming home, is he?"

"We're not sure," said Carmichael.

"He'll be glad to get out of here, I can tell you that. Hope you haven't taken his radio or anything again."

"No, I was off duty yesterday. I've only seen him this morning and he's told me he may be going home." She looked the girl up and down appraisingly and as she did so something caught her eye. Across the corner of the girl's coat down by the pocket was a smear of aluminium paint. She looked back at the girl's face, then at Doug's, then back to the girl.

"You've spoilt your nice coat. You've got some aluminium paint on it, at the bottom near the pocket."

The girl picked up the corner of her coat, looked at the paint, then a swift glance passed between her and Doug.

"Huh, must have got that painting your bike, Doug," she said.

Doug, obviously not so quick, answered, "What d'you mean . . . Nobody paints my bloody bike!" Then he stopped, getting the message a little late. "Oh, yeah, that's right," he said.

Carmichael looked at them both. She knew now. If she had doubted at all, she did so no longer. She was not going to hand such a slender piece of evidence to the police. Oh no, she was going to use it herself.

She sat down at her desk again and the two walked off, talking quietly as they went up the ward to see Leo. Carmichael's mind felt curiously at rest. She would deal with it somehow in her own way. She gazed at the white blotting paper in front of her, took up a pen and began to draw, quite meticulously, quite well, a picture of the lift doors.

CHAPTER 24

Carmichael longed to go home but half-dreaded it. She wanted so much to see if the cats had come back and, if they hadn't, she wanted to go on looking for them. When people spoke to her she did not, for seconds, recognize their faces. It was a horrible feeling, she remembered, and dreaded it. She knew only too well that depression did this to you. She tried to shake it off and an event that happened during the afternoon did something to help her.

The old lady in the women's ward, Mrs. Bradshaw, was more troublesome. Nurses went to her bedside several times and managed for the moment to calm the old lady, but as soon as they went away she started again and once started to climb over her cot sides. This brought Carmichael and she drew the curtains round the bed to shield the old lady from inquisitive stares. Mrs. Bradshaw fought feebly as Carmichael gently tried to make her lie back on the pillows. At last Carmichael sent a nurse to measure an injection for the old lady according to the prescription that Dr. Manning had written in her notes. When the nurse brought the syringe to the bedside Carmichael checked the injection and, with the nurse holding Mrs. Bradshaw's arm firmly, plunged the needle in, then told the nurse to wait by the patient until it took effect, to stay and hold her hand.

Carmichael sighed. The old lady had ousted the memory of her cottage and the cats, but only for a moment. As she walked through the ward carrying the kidney dish and the disposable syringe and went into the sluice to get rid of it, the full force of her problems rushed upon her. She went back and sat down in her office and was gazing in front of her abstractedly when Staff Nurse Minter came hurrying out of the men's ward, her face crimson. She came into Carmichael's office, entering it without ceremony.

"Those three, Sister, I've had enough of them. They're taking the other patient's fruit and throwing it about, rolling oranges up the floor. I really can't stand them any longer. The visitors don't like it. One man told Douglas off and the boy went up and nearly pushed the man over. We shall have to— What can we do, Sister? The visitors are frightened of them."

"I'll deal with it," said Carmichael. She marched into the ward and toward Leo Kalinsky's bed. As she did so Leo, who was walking about with the other two, suddenly slipped and crashed to the floor, falling on his bad elbow and uttering a howl of pain. Douglas was standing with an apple in his hand tossing it up and down. He stopped and looked down at Leo. The girl, a thin cigarette between her lips, bent down and looked too, then looked up accusingly as Carmichael approached.

"He fell. He's probably hurt his arm. He should be on the bed. He shouldn't be walking about. It's your fault. There's nobody supervising."

Carmichael helped Leo to his feet. He was clutching the plaster on his arm and tears now were streaming down his face. She pulled the curtains round the bed and helped him lie down. She looked at the plaster, which was badly cracked, and turned cold eyes on the other two.

"You have been throwing this fruit about and your friend has slipped on it." She pointed to the floor. "It's entirely your responsibility and I shall hold you to it."

The girl's eyes wavered for a moment and dropped before Carmichael's. Then she said defiantly:

"Well, he was chucking fruit about too. We were only trying to have a bit of fun to stir things up."

The boy threw the curtain aside at the end of the bed, walked across and put the apple he had been tossing in his hand down on a locker. Carmichael heard him say:

"There you are, old man, there's yer bloody apple back, and

if there's any more of yer stuff missing, well, it's at the top of the ward where we threw 'em. It won't have hurt 'em." He came back into the cubicle where Carmichael was still attending to Leo Kalinsky.

"You'd better go," she said. "I'll have to get Doctor to look at this plaster." She felt boiling with hatred. It was as much as she could do to speak coherently. She felt she didn't mind if Kalinsky's arm was hurt. He was one of those who would have behaved the same to her cats—tortured them, killed them if he'd had the chance. It was only that he had just happened to be in hospital and so had made her the target of these terrible young people's behaviour. She turned toward the other two and her look was so menacing that both Doug and Jane backed through the curtain.

"Cool it, Sister, we were only having a . . . just a bit of fun."

"Your bit of fun will probably mean that your friend's fracture has come to some harm and I'm not at all sure that I will be able to let him go home tomorrow."

"Oh, come on, it's nothing to do with you. It's what that Paki says or his boss."

"It's what the X-ray says," said Carmichael.

She moved forward and they backed rather uneasily before her. She followed them down the ward, out of the door, into the little foyer and out of the swing-doors. They made towards the lift. She said tersely:

"Stairs, not the lift, please. Stairs. You'll hear more of this."

For once they did not make towards the lift doors but started down the stairs. Half-way down Doug stopped, held on to the banister, and, swinging sideways against the wall, looked up at her, his eyes glittering with defiance:

"See that Paki gets it right, that's all. If Leo's done himself an injury, see he gets it right or . . ."

". . . or what?" said Carmichael. She felt completely unafraid of them, as though if they came back to her cottage tonight or any night she'd deal with them. If they came, she'd be there waiting with a knife. She'd kill them. She half-hoped they would come back. If her cats had gone, there was nothing else to live for. She would be pleased to dispose of them.

"Come on, Jane, leave her alone. Look at her, she looks real dotty."

They clattered away down the stairs out of sight, and Carmichael turned and went back through the swing-doors.

CHAPTER 25

Carmichael sat down in her office for a moment, covered her face with her hands, and tried to still her trembling, then picked up the phone and dialled Dr. Manning. She realized the blow Leo Kalinsky had taken on his plaster might well have dislodged the tricky reduction of his elbow injury and after all she was in charge and the patient must be dealt with.

"Dr. Manning," she said at last, "I wonder if you could come up to the men's orthopaedic? Yes, it is important. Thank you."

By the time Manning managed to get up to the orthopaedic ward half an hour later, the visitors had all gone. He came up the stairs, his white coat flying, his stethoscope round his neck, and went into Carmichael's office.

"What is it, Sister? I'm damn busy in Casualty. I'm doing two people's work, you know."

Carmichael, her temper still roused and her feelings almost uncontrollable, flashed back at him. "I would not have rung you, Dr. Manning, unless it was essential, you should know that. The boy, Leo Kalinsky, the elbow, he had a fall right onto the plaster. He's cracked it and I think the elbow will need to be X-rayed."

"Well, how did he fall, for goodness' sake?"

"If you really want to know, his two yobbo visitors were throwing fruit about and he slid on something."

Manning sighed. "All right, Sister, I'd better go and look at him."

They walked up the ward. The curtains were now drawn back and Leo Kalinsky lay looking wan against the pillows, still holding the plaster with his other hand. He turned to look at the doctor.

"Don't mess it about. It hurts, it hurts like hell," he said.

The house officer examined the plaster then shrugged his shoulders. "I'll write an X-ray form, Sister. He'll have to go down and get it X-rayed. He may well have done something to it. The plaster's broken, not cracked. You know what these fractures are, they slip awfully easily."

"You can say that again. It's hurting. Aren't you going to give me something for it?" said Leo, looking up white-faced at the doctor.

"Yes, I will."

"It was your own fault entirely." Carmichael's voice was acid. "I shall have to get someone to clear up this floor, and don't get out of bed until I've done so."

Leo didn't answer. Manning and Carmichael walked down the ward and she started again:

"Neither you nor Dr. Patel have done anything about old Mrs. Bradshaw. She kicked up an awful row during visiting time and upset the visitors in the women's ward. You could even hear her in the men's ward. It is too bad. Haven't you managed to find her a bed anywhere?"

"No, I haven't, Sister. I rang Annington and St. Fleets, and Patel's tried as well. They haven't got any beds, they're full. You know what it's like. I'll do something as soon as I can. Meanwhile, you'll just have to cope."

"Well, while you're here you'll have to write up another sedative for her. I've given the last one. She's all right now, but what about tonight? I don't like leaving night Staff Nurse with a problem like this, she'll have half the ward awake all night. She's getting worse, you know, climbing over the cot sides . . . and I don't have the staff to cope. She'll probably have another fall and break her other hip. You really must see to it." Carmichael's tone was venomous. All the hatred pent up inside her seemed to flow out onto the house officer.

He looked at her in surprise and resentment. "Well, it's no use speaking to me like that, Sister. I can't cope with everything, you know—I've got other things in the hospital to do—but I will try."

They walked into the office and Carmichael took out Mrs. Bradshaw's and Leo Kalinsky's notes and banged them down in front of him. He opened them and said more mildly:

"I'd better write up Leo Kalinsky's sedation and X-ray form first. He must get that done before they close. They leave at five, you know."

Carmichael walked out of the office. She felt she couldn't stay near anybody. She looked at her watch and saw it was nearly five. She would soon be off duty. Thank God for that.

One of the nurses came up to her. "They haven't sent the butter up, Sister."

Carmichael flashed round at her. "Well, do something about it, then. Ring the kitchen."

The nurse, somewhat dismayed, went up to the wall phone and Carmichael realized that normally she would not have let a junior nurse phone the kitchen, but today she did not feel like herself, she felt like some other person, a person full of hatred and depression. She suddenly felt she would slip home early, a thing she never did. She stopped Staff Nurse Minter, who was hurrying into the women's ward.

"I told nurse to ring about the butter."

"The butter?" Minter looked puzzled.

"Yes. They haven't sent it up so I've told her to ring the kitchen. See that it comes. I'm going early, Staff Nurse. I've got a splitting headache."

"You look as if you have, Sister. You're as white as a sheet. Why don't you go now?" said Minter sympathetically.

Carmichael could not stand even that. "I'll go when I'm ready, Staff Nurse, and not before," she said, and Minter, her lips puckered up in a half whistle, went on her way.

"I suppose it's the cottage and everything," she whispered in the direction of the house officer, who was still busily writing in the office.

He looked up. "What did you say, Staff?"

"Nothing," said Minter, then turned to a nurse passing.

"Don't go near Sister Carmichael, not at the moment. If you've got any problems, come to me, right?"

"I've got a problem," answered the nurse. "Old Mrs. Bradshaw's started threshing about again and she only had that injection a bit ago during visitors and I've got to do a bedpan round, so I can't keep an eye on her."

She hurried away, young and harassed, and Minter looked after her, smiling. She'd gone through that period long ago, the feeling that the whole responsibility of the ward rested on your shoulders, mostly because you seemed to be the one that got told off if anything happened that shouldn't. She shrugged and went into the women's ward and walked along towards Mrs. Bradshaw's bed.

Dr. Manning came out of the office and handed Carmichael the X-ray form.

"Get it done as soon as you can and ring me. I'll come up from Casualty and have a look at it, or you can send a nurse down with the X-ray and I could see it down there—that would help."

"What nurse? I'm short, Doctor, I've not got anyone to send running around the hospital looking for you."

"No one has to look for me, Sister. I'm in Casualty and shall be there for the rest of the evening," said Manning rather bitterly.

"I'll send the orderly down with it, then, that is if she comes on. You'll have to let me know what it's like. He's going home tomorrow, you know, if he's all right, that is, and if he isn't, well . . ."

"Right, Sister."

Dr. Manning admired Carmichael's efficiency, but he was also obviously a little riled by her attitude this afternoon and he left looking ruffled, pushing the swing-doors open in front of him, then going over to the lift and punching the button. Nothing happened, no lift arrived, and he started to run down the stairs.

CHAPTER 26

Carmichael put her hand to her forehead and held it there for a moment. Her hand was cold but her forehead was hot and her eyes sore and aching. It was lack of sleep, she supposed. She'd got to get home. She went into her office and picked up her handbag. She'd said something about going to Nurse Minter, hadn't she? Yes, she was sure she had. She would go now. She hesitated. Perhaps she'd better tell Miss O'Donoghue she was going home. She rang the front hall and asked them to bleep Miss O'Donoghue.

"Miss O'Donoghue has gone. It's nearly five, Sister."

"Oh, of course, I forget these nine-to-five administrative jobs can close down promptly on time." Carmichael's voice was sarcastic and suddenly she didn't care at all whether whoever was acting for Miss O'Donoghue knew that she had gone. She would just leave. Minter must handle things as best she could. Anyway, the male nurse was on at six, so she had less than an hour to cope on her own.

"There's the form, Staff Nurse. Get Leo down to X-ray. They sometimes don't go until quarter or half past five, but I think that's too much to hope for today. Anyway, if they've all gone you must get someone back. Take him in a chair—he looks pretty white—and then get the orderly when she comes on to take the X-ray down to Dr. Manning in Casualty, or get him up here. He'll have to look at it and if it's displaced the fracture will just have to be done again. It's the boy's own fault."

"Yes, Sister." Minter obviously thought it was better to say nothing else. Carmichael was about to make her way through the swing-doors when a nurse ran downstairs in theatre garb, short green dress, paper hat pulled over her dark curls, one tendril escaping at the back, her mask hanging round her neck. She came clomping along in her white rubber boots.

"Oh, Sister Carmichael, what an afternoon! The lift has packed up! It's been dodgy all day but now it won't go at all. I've rung the electrician. He had to come to the theatre this afternoon, the diathermy went on the blink. There's a jinx on this afternoon."

"I've been complaining about that lift. What's he going to do?"

"He reckons the circuit's gone. We can't use it and I've got to come down and tie the doors up. He's bringing OUT OF ORDER notices. There's a patient upstairs. Luckily it's only a minor op but we've got to get a porter to manhandle him down the stairs. I've come down to warn the wards and tie up the lift doors."

"Well, don't go into the wards in that garb. Tell Staff Nurse Minter to see the lift doors are tied. I don't know how a hospital like this can have such a primitive . . ." Her voice failed her.

"Comic, isn't it, Sister, but I've got to get bandages from the wards to do it." The junior nurse suddenly burst out laughing. "Awful, isn't it, though, Sister? Well, we won't be able to operate tomorrow if it's not mended, so the electrician is coming back to see what he can do. He's off, of course, it's overtime but . . . Lucky for him, I said, but he didn't agree."

Carmichael hardly listened to this. She continued on downstairs to the changing-room and then home to misery—but perhaps, perhaps they were there.

Staff Nurse Minter greeted the theatre nurse with surprise:

"What are you doing here dressed like that? Good job Sister's not here to see you."

"I've just seen her outside. She didn't say anything. It's the lift, it's not working. The electrician is coming—ten minutes, he said—poor devil, he's been in the theatre already this afternoon coping with the diathermy. I told Sister Carmichael we've got to tie the lift doors up. Can I have a crêpe bandage, or one or two, please. I should have brought some with me."

"All right, but try not to be so forgetful," said Staff Nurse Minter automatically. She'd met this junior nurse before. She went into the sluice-room, opened a drawer, and took out some four-inch crêpe bandages and brought them back.

"Those all right?" she asked. "They're old ones and if they're stained it doesn't matter, does it."

The nurse nodded gratefully. "The electrician's coming with OUT OF ORDER notices. He said he'd be here in a few minutes."

She went out followed by Minter, who watched her bind the two handles of the wooden doors together firmly and then knot the bandage.

She turned rather helplessly to Minter. "I have to use these as well. I'm supposed to do them on all the floors, do you mind? You see, it's dangerous. I mean, if someone opened the door—well, you'd just go hurtling down and be raspberry jam at the bottom."

"Well, for goodness' sake get on with it. Yes, you can have those bandages," said the Staff Nurse. "I've got a patient to take to X-ray in a wheelchair. How am I supposed to do that, can you tell me?"

"Ask one of the porters," said the young nurse. "He'll have to . . . I don't know how we'll manage. Serve them right for not putting a new lift in."

She went off downstairs laughing gaily, the bandages in her hand to secure the lift doors on the other floors. She dropped one on the first flight of stairs and it opened and rolled down the stairs. She looked back at Minter and grimaced. Then the Staff Nurse heard her suddenly greet someone.

"Oh, I'm glad you've come with your notices. OUT OF ORDER should be put on that lift the whole damn time. What are you going to do up there? There's a patient—well, only a minor op, but how's he going to get down the stairs? He's still woozy."

"Nothing to do with me," said a gruff voice. "I've got

enough problems with the electrical equipment in this damn hospital. What an afternoon!"

Staff Nurse Minter stopped there for a couple of minutes, listening, the electrician ascending, nurse descending. As he reached her floor he looked at her.

"Well, what have you got to grumble about? Don't say anything has gone wrong on your ward."

"No, I was just talking to Nurse. She was tying up the doors for you."

"Oh, big deal." He hung a large notice on the brass handle of the doors. "I've got a damn good mind to leave it like that for the night," he said, "but I know I'll get the push if I do. I'll have to get the other chap and we'll work on it. The circuit's gone, I suppose—the whole bloody thing. Well, you'd know it would."

"Can you repair it? I mean in time for ops tomorrow," asked Minter.

The man shook his head dubiously. "I dunno. Can't say with a set-up as old as this. It's only about two weeks, you know, before they put the new one in."

"I didn't know that. Nobody ever tells you anything," said Minter.

"I knew it wouldn't last out, this one."

His expression was bitter, he wanted to get off duty, Minter diagnosed. She knew the feeling.

"It's all very well to say that overtime is well paid, but I don't want their bloody overtime. I was going to the dogs tonight," he continued, then went upstairs towards the theatre, the last notice dangling from his hand.

Minter turned back into the ward to her problems, to see if the butter had come, to see if old Mrs. Bradshaw had settled, to see how she was going to get Leo Kalinsky down to X-ray with no lift. She sighed. There was a lot of sighing being done on the orthopaedic ward today. She went through the doors and they swung to behind her.

CHAPTER 27

Carmichael arrived home in the cheerless autumn evening, drove rapidly, almost carelessly, into her garage, did not stop to lock the car but rushed to the front door, her hand trembling so violently she dropped the key, retrieved it, and with difficulty inserted it into the new lock. She flung open the door, then stopped. There was no sound, no welcoming miaow.

She hated the thought of the evening. She could not be sure that the cats were not somewhere suffering, and she could picture them wandering about in some strange part of the village, bleeding, crying. She tried to dismiss the thought—she could feel it bringing on the old despair, the old dark cloud.

Instead of getting herself a meal, she spent the evening again in the darkening garden. She was glad she had no near neighbours, they would think her mad. At last she went back into the house to make herself tea. She'd just put the kettle on when the telephone rang. That startled her, for her phone seldom rang.

"Hallo." Her voice sounded hoarse and peculiar even to her own ears, but the voice at the other end was familiar.

"Oh, Sister Carmichael, is that you?"

"Yes."

"It didn't sound like you. It sounded as if you'd got a cold."

It was Mrs. Sampson.

"No, I'm all right. I've been out looking for them again this evening. I left the trapdoor open all day, of course, but there's no sign of them."

"I'm sorry, Sister. It's rotten for you. I know what I would feel like. The only thing is, I've heard something."

Carmichael's heart leaped. "What, Mrs. Sampson? What have you heard?"

"Well, I'm not sure . . . There's a cottage about a mile up the lane from here, it's an awful little lane, but you might be able to get the car up there. An old lady lives in the cottage and the postman said that she'd taken in a cat, a stray. I don't like telling you, but the postman said it had had its tail cut off. Vandals had done it, I suppose. Anyway, she's taken it in and it's all right, but I wondered . . ."

"What colour is it? What's the cat like?"

"I didn't ask. I didn't think to. What with the inquest and everything, it just didn't occur to me. I've had a letter from our . . . But that doesn't matter. The point is, the postman delivered that and he told me about the cat. I never thought to ask what the cat was like."

"Is she . . . is the old lady on the telephone?" Carmichael asked.

"No, no, I shouldn't think so."

"I'll go straight away. Thank you for thinking of me with all your trouble, thank you for letting me know." Carmichael was breathless with agitation and hope.

Mrs. Sampson had described the way to get to the old lady's cottage, and Carmichael thought, as far as she could remember, it was almost a track, but that didn't matter, she'd take the car across a ploughed field if necessary. She used to be so fastidious about the car, always wiping it down when she brought it in if it had been raining, even hosing the wheels if they were muddy, but all that fussiness had been swept away by this disaster.

She went out, locked the front door, got into her car, switched on the engine, then the lights. They lighted up a misty rain as she drove out. It had not been raining when she had come home. It had been dismal, dull, but not raining. Now as she set off along the lane, going slowly so that she wouldn't miss the turning, the rain increased.

She saw a light in Mrs. Sampson's cottage, a light also in Mrs. Pilcher's next door. She drove on, the rain lessening a little, and soon Carmichael was able to turn off the windscreen wipers. The countryside was suddenly lighted by the clouds leaving the face of the moon, letting it shine down benignly. Carmichael motored on and then saw a silhouette against the moonlit sky, a small cottage. She stopped. There were asters in the garden like she had in front of her cottage. She walked up the path to the door and looked for a bell or a knocker, but there was none. She tapped on the wooden door and it opened almost at once. A fat old lady stood in front of her and she reminded Carmichael of Mrs. Jenks. That and the rain stopping and the moon appearing seemed to Carmichael to be good omens.

"The cat, the cat you found. Mrs. Sampson, she telephoned me. I thought I'd . . ." The old woman nodded and beckoned her inside.

"Poor little soul. Have you lost yours?" she asked. "Well, I won't use bad language, miss, but someone had cut her tail off. It hadn't been run over, I'm sure. I think it had been cut off. Anyway, she's all right now. I bandaged it up. It wasn't bleeding, it was just as if it had been cut off with scissors—at least that's what I think." The word "she" had made Carmichael more optimistic. She dared not ask the colour of the cat but followed the old lady through into the minuscule sitting-room. There, sitting in front of the fire, was a cat, a white bandage round the end of its tail, which flicked slightly as it turned its green eyes towards Carmichael. Her heart sank—the cat was coal black.

"That's not yours, is it?" the old lady said. She could tell by Carmichael's downcast expression. "I'm sorry in one way, glad in another. That's life, isn't it? I don't think she's very young, and she'd go home if she lived round here. If she doesn't want to go home, I shall keep her."

"Yes, of course." Carmichael bent down and stroked the cat but it flinched away from her.

"Will you have a cup of tea or anything? I mean, it's so disappointing for you coming out on a night like this and then finding it's not yours. I don't see many people up here, not this time of night—not that I'd open the door after what you hear, especially after your break-in. It frightened me. It's fate, I suppose. I said to myself, I've lived here for fifty years and nothing like that has happened about here before. Perhaps they thought you had something valuable? I haven't, not even a telly. Don't want one. I like the wireless, though." She chatted on as she saw Carmichael to the door.

Carmichael could not even answer her about the cup of tea or tell her about her cats. Her disappointment was overwhelming.

She thanked the old woman and went back to her car and drove home. She was glad that the cat was being looked after, but if only it had been . . . Supposing they had done that to hers, cut . . . She tried to dismiss the thought. Each time she got back to her cottage she had this feeling that she felt was stupid, that they'd be there, but of course they were not. She was met only by silence.

At the open front door she turned round and looked down the garden. It was bathed in moonlight, the asters gleaming palely. Suddenly she hated it, hated the garden, the cottage, the trees at the back, everything that she'd loved so much. Those two, Douglas and Jane, had made her hate it. Well, she would do something about it, she didn't know what. She remembered the girl's face, her purple lips, and then the smudge of aluminium paint on her coat. Oh yes, she would do something about it. They had murdered her cats and she—she'd settle with them.

Carmichael didn't go to bed that night until about three. There was little question of going to sleep. For a long time before she went upstairs she sat in deep depression, which she was more and more afraid would put her back into the psychiatric ward. She fell asleep in the chair at last and woke stiff and cold, then went up to her bed. She got up at five o'clock, went down to the kitchen and made more tea, opening the back door wide. Dawn had not even broken yet. She drank her tea, leaning tiredly against the sink, watching the horizon. The sky began to streak with grey. The dawn, she thought, another day without them. She would go upstairs, have a bath, and get back on duty. Duty in a way was better than being here, and yet in another way it was not.

CHAPTER 28

Carmichael was on duty at eleven and didn't leave the ward until half past eight.

When she had arrived at the hospital and changed into uniform, she went upstairs to the ward and noticed that the lift doors were still bound up with the crêpe bandage that the nurse had put on yesterday afternoon and a big OUT OF ORDER notice was now hanging from the handles.

Geoffrey Miles greeted her as she came through the swing-doors:

"Good morning, Sister. I expect you noticed the lift is still not working. We've had the hospital secretary here and everybody else it seems, but what can they do, the circuit's gone or something. The men are up there." He pointed theatrewards. "I can't see they can do much. They've cancelled the gynae list. I'm glad it isn't Mr. Dalby's day. He wouldn't have been best pleased, would he?"

Carmichael looked at him blankly, her mind not yet oriented to the hospital. She was still back at the cottage in the garden, looking. She dragged herself to the present.

"It's disgraceful, I think, disgraceful that a hospital like this . . ."

"Well, it's the money, isn't it? We've had to wait so long for the new lift. Still, it will soon be here. It's just a case of getting this working till it comes, I suppose. The new lift, that'll be posh enough. We won't be able to see who's using it, either. I hear it's one of those closed ones." Then he looked more serious and said, "Have you found your cats, Sister?"

Carmichael shook her head, rather surprised that he should

have asked. "No, I think they've gone for good. I think those vandals did something to them."

"Gone for good . . . You mean, run away or . . ." He obviously did not like to say the next word and Carmichael supplied it for him, but perhaps it was not the word he was going to use.

". . . been killed by those . . ."

"Yes."

She could not go on, her voice thickened and Geoffrey Miles looked slightly embarrassed and turned away, saying as he did so:

"That old Mrs. Bradshaw . . . oh dear, she's been a trial in the night. According to the night nurse she kept everybody awake again, yelling and screaming as if she wanted to tell somebody something, but the nurse couldn't get it out of her, whatever it was. She's quiet for the moment, she's had another sedative. Dr. Patel came up earlier. I told him we couldn't go on like this and he'd just have to get her transferred. He's trying—well, he says he is—and, oh, I nearly forgot, Mr. Parsons may do a round this morning."

"*May* do a round, Staff Nurse?" Carmichael said.

"Yes. Well, you know what Mr. Parsons is like—not like Mr. Dalby."

"Very well, then. I hope Mrs. Bradshaw is making the same noise when he comes. Perhaps he'll realize how it's disturbing his patients. It will at least prove that we're not over-reacting."

"Yes. She's very disturbed. I've tried, and so have the other nurses, to understand, but we've had no luck. Oh, here comes your coffee, Sister."

Carmichael looked up surprised as the orderly brought in her coffee and put it on her desk.

"Thought you'd like this, Sister. Have you found them?"

Carmichael shook her head. Myrtle, the orderly, was a nice woman, but as usual Carmichael kept aloof from her. In her opinion, as Sister she had to, although she knew some of the Sisters were more friendly, went out with their orderlies, took them home in their cars sometimes, but not Carmichael. This cup of coffee, however, and the concern for her cats warmed her a little.

"Thank you, Myrtle. No, they haven't come back," she said with an effort.

"Well, I'm sorry about that, Sister. Don't like cats meself, I think they're cruel devils. Still, I know you're fond of them and I'm sorry."

Carmichael did not answer and the orderly walked back into the kitchen, Carmichael noting with some disfavour that her grey hair, done up in an untidy bun, was constantly falling down in wisps on the back of her collar. She must tell her about it, but not now.

She sat down and wondered what to do. That was something she had never done before. She would go through the procedure sheets, the off-duty rotas, check the report, goodness knows there was enough to do, but this depression . . . She sipped the coffee and looked at the outside of the report book for some time, then reluctantly opened it. She scanned the report—comfortable, comfortable, comfortable. There was nothing much said about patients who were progressing satisfactorily. Then she came to Leo Kalinsky. His X-ray report showed a re-fracture, bone in alignment, arm replastered in present position. She called Geoffrey Miles back into her office.

"Staff Nurse, what's this? Did he have to have the arm re-reduced?"

"Well, not exactly, Sister. They thought the arm had re-fractured in the same place, but it had not moved. Anyway, they took the plaster off—it was cracked—and replastered it and he's got to stay in for another few days, then have a re-X-ray and see if it's moved. Stupid little fool, mucking about like that. That lumbers us with him longer. I mean, those mates of his will be back and making trouble again. Well, if you don't mind, Sister, I'd like to tell him he's to stay in bed while they are here. After all, if he gets to the rest-room, God knows what they'll get up to and he might fall again."

Carmichael agreed. "Yes, yes, when they come he must stay

in bed and the two of them can sit by the bed and talk to him. That is all I'll allow."

"Allow, Sister! It's hard enough to make them do anything. They seem to have no respect for authority at all."

"They're not due here till this afternoon, so let's worry about it when it happens."

Geoff Miles nodded and padded off to the men's ward.

Mr. Parsons's round was done with his usual geniality. He promised to speak to Dr. Patel and Dr. Manning about Mrs. Bradshaw, although she wasn't his patient. He stood by the old woman's bed and she looked at him with rheumy eyes.

"I'm frightened it'll starve," she said suddenly in her husky voice which could rise to such shrill heights when she became irrational. At the moment she seemed fairly lucid. She was determined to talk to Mr. Parsons or anybody.

He moved nearer the bed. *"Who* will starve, Mrs. Bradshaw?" he asked kindly, casting a quick glance towards Carmichael, who also drew nearer.

"Me cat, Fluffy. She's at the cottage, see. Well, there's no one there, there's nobody who'll feed her. Me cat," her voice rose to a wail.

Carmichael looked at Mr. Parsons and Mr. Parsons looked back at her, shrugged his shoulders, and arched his eyebrows.

"Her cat, is it?" He turned again to the old lady. "I expect one of the neighbours will feed it."

The old lady shook her head wildly from side to side. "Me neighbour won't. She's 'orrible, me neighbour. She'll starve, she's just starving, I know."

"Cats hunt birds and mice. She'll be all right."

Mr. Parsons put his arm kindly round the old woman's shoulders but she shook it off.

"She can't, she can't. She's blind, she can't see." Again her voice rose to a near scream and some of the other old ladies rose on their elbows to see what was happening.

"Well." Mr. Parsons looked rather helplessly at Carmichael, but she was not looking at him, she was gazing in front of her, thinking that cats seemed to inhabit her life at the moment, now a blind one. For some reason she thought of Harry, how Harry had had to move about the house carefully, but he was always supplied with food. Suddenly she went close to the bedside and bent down.

"I'll go and look for your cat. I'll find her, I'll feed her." She said it in such a way that the Consultant looked at her rather strangely and then quickly adjusted his expression as she looked at him.

"That's very, very kind of you, Sister," he said. "Where does Mrs. Bradshaw live?"

Carmichael looked up at him, her eyes curiously blank, and she answered, "I don't know. I'll look it up in her notes and I'll find the place." She spoke positively. After all, Tibbles and Torty, one of them might have been somehow blinded. Suppose they had thrown something at the cats. She sat down suddenly on the locker, again feeling sick and faint.

Mr. Parsons came round the bed. "Put your head down between your knees, Sister," he said, and she did so, putting her hand up to stop her paper cap moving. She felt better after a moment or two.

"Are you all right, Sister? You've had some trouble lately, with some burglars, was it? Somebody told me—Mr. Dalby, I think."

"Yes, I have, sir, yes."

The blinded cat still seemed to roam in front of her eyes as she felt Mr. Parsons's kind hand on her shoulder. It was the cat she saw in front of her eyes, blind, the sockets of the eyes red.

She turned to Mrs. Bradshaw. "Is Fluffy tabby and white?" she asked. The old woman looked up at her in surprise.

"Yes. Do you know her then, Sister, have you seen her?"

Carmichael shook her head and walked away from the bed, folllowed by Mr. Parsons, still asking her if she felt better. She did. What little colour she had, had come back to her cheeks.

"Yes, thank you, sir, I'm all right now. I'm sorry I . . ." she said and followed him politely through the swing-doors and out of the ward. She held the door open and he turned to her.

"Damn nuisance this lift. My operating day tomorrow and I won't be able to do it. Still, that'll make a rest." He smiled at her. "Take care of yourself, Sister. Have a little drop of the ward brandy."

Carmichael smiled absently at him, looked at her watch and saw it was lunch-time. She didn't feel like any lunch but she would go down and have some. Perhaps the faintness was due to the fact that she couldn't remember when she had last eaten.

In the dining-room she mechanically ate the food, surrounded by Sisters who were talking animatedly about the lift, or lack of it.

"They were supposed to be getting them back into working order by tomorrow."

"Bet they won't. There's always a piece that they can't get. Anyway, the age that lift is, you can't wonder."

"Still, we shall have the new one in soon," said a more optimistic Sister.

"There's nothing we can do about it. It's a shame, though, the ops can't be done."

"I heard that they're going to use Out Patients theatre, or try to for the minors."

"Yes, they're doing a big clean down there and stocking it up a bit. That'll please Sister Hill."

They all laughed but Carmichael did not join in. She went on eating her lunch, then, without speaking, got up and went to the Sisters' rest-room. She heard one of her colleagues remark as she left the table:

"Old Carmichael's badly hit, you know, by that burglary."

"It's her cats," said another. "It's her cats, you see, that's all she's got. What she wants is a man."

Carmichael shuddered as she made her way out of the dining-room upstairs to the rest-room for coffee.

CHAPTER 29

The rest of the afternoon passed slowly for Carmichael. At three o'clock the visitors poured up the stairs bearing their gifts of cakes, flowers, Lucozade, and other bottles of soft drinks. They all nodded and smiled at Carmichael, but Carmichael hardly looked at them. She did not encourage them to come in and ask her questions, and if she looked at them they might start to do so.

"When will Granny be able to go home?" or "Grandad says his back's sore. He's not getting bedsores, is he, Sister?" or "We can't possibly have her home, Sister. We haven't got the room. And anyway, she upsets the children," or "Sister, he says his knee is more painful and it's not being done. What's happening?"

She beckoned to Staff Nurse Minter, who was now on duty.

"Staff Nurse," she said, "go round and answer any queries. I don't feel awfully well."

"You don't look it, Sister. You should be off duty. You should have had three or four days after that lot."

Carmichael stopped her irritably. "I prefer to be here rather than at home," she said. "Now please do as I say. Answer any questions as best you can and come to me if there is anything complicated."

She determinedly drew the report book towards her. She wanted to read it more carefully. It was ridiculous just skimming over everything because her mind felt so strange. She must pull herself together, and tonight . . . But her mind turned away from tonight. She must stop this searching and rest. Suddenly she decided what she would do. She would not go straight home. She couldn't bear it anymore, this rushing home to see if the cats were there. It was useless, anyway. No, she would go to the old woman's place, Mrs. Bradshaw's. It was moonlight, or it had been last night, so it probably would be tonight. She would go and look for the blind cat and look for Harry. She was suddenly aware of what she had said in her mind, "would go and look for Harry." That was a strange thing to think. The cat's name was . . . what was it? Fluffy.

She pulled her mind back and concentrated on the report book. This time she managed to take in everything. She turned the page and put today's date at the head, so that it would be ready when the report came to be written this evening, about seven-thirty after she had been to the staff dining-room for dinner. Yes, she would go to the Sisters' dining-room, she would eat her dinner. She must get back to normal. She would never see her cats again, she knew it now. She put her hands up to her face and the tears fell into her cupped fingers.

Staff Nurse Minter managed to stave off most of the inquiries and Carmichael hardly had to speak to any of the visitors. One woman did put her head round the door, and she met Carmichael's irritable stare out of red-rimmed eyes. She looked at her curiously and said:

"I've brought you these, Sister. I heard you had a rotten time with the burglary and everything." She took the paper off a bundle of red cabbage-roses and offered them to Carmichael almost timidly.

"Timmy—I mean Timothy, my son—he's doing ever so well—with his knee, I mean. You are all ever so good to him . . . These are the last roses in my garden."

"Thank you." Carmichael took the proffered roses and looked at them. They were pretty, perfumed. "Thank you," she said again, and as she said it the curious coincidences went through her mind—the blind cat, the roses, and she remembered again Harry's flowers, roses too.

"It's all right, Sister," said the woman, and she hastily went through the swing-doors and away.

Visiting time was over. You could hear them clattering down the stairs. It was four-thirty. Carmichael left her office, put the flowers in a vase, placed them on her desk, and went to have her tea. This sequence of meals was, in a way, comforting. She was soon back looking more cheerful and went in the ward to supervise the round of backs and bedpans. She felt more herself. Maybe it was the thought of doing something, finding Fluffy. She felt quite sure that she'd find her, quite sure. It must be tonight. She would drive to the other side of town. She knew the place vaguely. She fancied there was a row of cottages and couldn't understand why the cat was not being looked after. Perhaps it was. Perhaps it was all nonsense. After all, the old lady was a bit confused, and as if to prove it Mrs. Bradshaw suddenly let out a banshee scream, then another. Carmichael hurried into the ward to try and calm the old lady, who was busy throwing the covers off her skinny legs.

"All right, all right, Mrs. Bradshaw."

Another nurse was already beside her, but Mrs. Bradshaw had knocked the nurse's cap sideways and was still struggling to get up.

"Isn't she awful, Sister. I wish she'd stop. Can I go to tea now, please?"

"Yes, Nurse, and don't speak like that in front of the patient. She has her lucid moments, you know. Put your cap on straight."

"Yes, Sister. Sorry, Sister. She bit me when I was feeding her this lunch-time. You can go off people, you know, that's what I said to her."

The nurse smiled. She was pretty and young and fresh and to Carmichael she looked like she had no cares, which is how Carmichael usually saw youth—trouble free.

"All right, Nurse, off you go, and send another nurse in to help me."

Seven o'clock came and Carmichael went to her dinner. It was nicer than usual—pork chop and decent vegetables and a good sweet. In fact, Carmichael ate it all with appetite. On the way back to her ward, she realized she was feeling more optimistic, ready to cope . . . with what? She thought of Harry. Where did he come in? Why Harry? Oh, of course, the blind cat, the roses. How had she known what the cat looked like—tabby and white? Perhaps Mrs. Bradshaw had told her? No, she was sure she hadn't. She just knew. And the roses—it was as if Harry was calling her as she'd called to her cats. I'll find Fluffy. This time I won't make a mistake like I did with Harry. Carmichael felt with apprehension the strange feeling she had felt before come over her, the strange, familiar feeling . . .

She entered the ward to be met by an infuriated Staff Nurse.

"They're here. They say they can't help it whether it's visiting time or not. They just marched in. They said they'd got two friends coming in too. I can't do anything with them, Sister Carmichael, I really can't. They're all smoking again. I kept Leo in bed. I told him he was not to get out, and he hasn't. I think his arm hurts him a bit, and serve him right."

All this burst from Staff Nurse, who was usually a calm and efficient girl. Carmichael spoke quietly, shaking off her feeling of disorientation:

"I'll deal with them, Nurse, don't worry."

This, Carmichael decided, was the final confrontation she would have with this pair. She would get out of them what she could and then she would do something. Her confidence flowed back, her feeling of disorientation retreated. She marched into the ward, her head high, her shoulders back. She was herself again, the self she knew and recognized, all-powerful.

CHAPTER 30

Carmichael walked purposefully up the ward and an old man, Mr. Marks, put up his hand to stop her. She walked towards his bed, not able in her present mood to pass by a patient who called her.

"Yes, Mr. Marks, what can I do for you?" she asked.

"I told my wife this afternoon that I'm going home on Tuesday. She's worried that she won't be able to manage. She's wondering if I can get up the stairs. I told her I could."

Carmichael gazed at him and tried to smile reassuringly, but her mouth would not twist into the required shape. She answered:

"Tomorrow we'll get the medical social worker to have a chat with you about your stairs and everything. Don't worry."

She turned away but the old man wanted to go on talking and started again. Carmichael, however, had already left him and she could feel his eyes watching her resentfully as she made her way to Leo Kalinsky's bed.

When she got there she realized she was shaking again, not with fear this time but with anger. She stood at the end of the bed, grasped the rail at the foot, and looked down and saw that her knuckles were gleaming white, but it did something to still this shaking. The boy Doug had just taken a long drag on what was left of a cigarette. Carmichael looked at him and saw the smoke disappear like a white ball into his mouth and he closed his lips firmly over it.

Pot, she thought and the sweet smell that reached her confirmed it. The boy held the roach down between himself and the girl who was sitting next to him on the stool she'd dragged from under the bed, and the smoke spiralled up into the ward air.

"This is not visiting time, and in any case you're not supposed to smoke in the ward. No visitor smokes in the ward. You should know that by now. Haven't you caused enough trouble for your friend here?" She inclined her head towards Leo, who was lying propped up on his good arm, his eyes round, watching her.

"Oh, sorry, Sister, didn't know the times, you see. Nobody gave us a list or anything. We thought it was tonight and the smoke . . . Oh, well, we were only having a drag." It was the girl who spoke and she put what was left of the cigarette into her mouth and drew on it hard. The end glowed red and then she dropped it on the floor and ground it in with her booted foot, the high heel making a squeaking noise on the floor.

"Don't do that!" Carmichael's voice was sharp and the girl looked at her.

"Oh, sorry. Can't do anything right with you, Sister, can we?"

Carmichael stood for a moment, seconds only, though it seemed a long, long time before she said what she had to say. The girl's eyes appeared not to be focussing properly and Carmichael barked out the question at her suddenly:

"What did you do to my cats?"

The girl's lips widened and she showed her white teeth and giggled. "Tied their tails together, so one's walking backwards."

The boy, almost before she had got the sentence out, gave her a jab in the ribs with his elbow. "Shut up, Jane, you bloody fool," he said.

If Carmichael had needed any more proof, she had it now. She let go of the rail at the end of the bed and moved a little closer to the girl.

"Is that what you did? I see. Well, you'll be sorry for it, you'll regret it—then it will be too late."

Carmichael didn't know at the time what she meant, but it

satisfied her to see a sudden flash of fear in the girl's eyes. She turned her head a little and looked at Doug and then at Leo.

"You had better tell your visitors to go or I'll have to get someone to evict them."

Carmichael turned on her heel and walked away. You couldn't tie two cats' tails together, of that she was certain, and anyway, if that's all they had done, the cats would have set up an outcry, surely. She walked on down the ward, conscious that she was weaving a little. She couldn't walk completely straight and she wasn't sure why. She didn't feel giddy. She arrived at the door, paused for a moment, and one of her nurses went by and said:

"You all right, Sister? You do look pale."

"I'm all right, Nurse," said Carmichael and started across what seemed an interminable journey to her office where she could sit down. She sank into her chair but she couldn't think. Someone came to the door and spoke to her and she remembered saying something. It must have been the right remark as the person went away apparently satisfied. She looked down at her blotting-pad and there, neatly drawn by herself, was the picture of the lift doors. She suddenly steadied, got up, went to the door of the men's ward and looked in. The boy and the girl were showing some signs of leaving. Doug was standing talking to Leo, the girl had picked up her handbag and was tightening the scarf at her neck, but she was still seated.

Carmichael looked round. Two of her nurses had gone to supper, the other one was in the women's ward—she could hear the talking—otherwise, the wards were fairly silent. Suddenly Mrs. Bradshaw broke the silence with one of her strange cries. Carmichael thought hazily, I must ring Dr. Patel, but she had something else to do before that.

She became suddenly purposeful, sure and calm. She went through the swing-doors. There was not a soul outside. From the theatres upstairs you could usually hear faint noises, but of course there was no operating. She looked through the two glass holes in the lift doors. They were blank, blank and empty. The lift, she knew, was stranded up on the theatre floor above. Deliberately and without haste she took off the large notice DANGER, OUT OF ORDER, stood it on the floor at her feet, then carefully unwrapped the bandage from the door handles. This took some little time, as the nurse from the theatre had knotted it securely. She pushed the unwound bandage into her pocket, picked up the notice and walked back to her office and slipped it under her blotting-pad, then she sat down in her chair and waited. She had not long to wait. Only about a couple of minutes went by when the two of them came through the door of the ward, went by her office, and the girl threw her a sardonic "Good night, Sister."

Carmichael looked up levelly and said, "Good night, but please don't take the lift, take the stairs. You're not supposed to take the lift, so behave yourselves for once." She said it in her most schoolmistressy tone, and instant rebellion came over the faces of both.

"We'll do what we bloody well like—we're sick of you," said Doug, and the girl broke in:

"We're the do-as-you-like gang, know us?"

She still looked slightly woozy and Carmichael wondered momentarily whether she took anything else besides pot. Carmichael noticed that as the girl walked out she was still gesticulating wildly and talking in a high, excited voice. As the swing-doors closed behind them, she heard them laughing again.

Carmichael waited a second or two. Those last remarks surely had been enough. Even so, she felt she must make sure, and she rose from her office chair, walked to the swing-doors and opened them. The two were just moving toward the lift doors and Doug had his hand on one of the brass handles.

"The stairs, I said the stairs," she called.

"Drop dead," said the girl, and the boy looked back in acknowledgement of the remark. They pulled open the doors and moved forward, still defiantly looking back at her. Then they stepped into blackness. Mrs. Bradshaw screamed. How lucky, Carmichael thought, it just covered nicely the . . . She went across and closed the lift doors, went unhurriedly back to her office, took the notice from under her blotting-pad, looked round carefully—no one. She went out again to the lift, wound the crêpe bandage round the handles, tying the knot firmly. Then she slipped the notice OUT OF ORDER over one handle, stilled its swinging, and went back. She sat down and drew her report book toward her. Staff Nurse Miles passing, looked at her industriously writing her report.

"Better put something about our Mrs. Bradshaw, Sister, she's at it again. Is she due for anything?"

Carmichael looked up at him. "Due for anything?" she said, and her voice was calm and even.

"Any more sedative, I mean."

"Yes, she is, but we'd better leave it for the night nurse to give later. If I give it now it means she can't have any more for four hours and the other patients won't get to sleep if she starts up then. She'll have to be moved. I thought . . ." The blind cat went through her mind, and again a feeling of disorientation came over her. "No, we'll leave her, I think. If she wants to make a noise, it's better she does it early." She looked at her watch. "You're nearly due off, aren't you, Staff Nurse?"

"Yes," Miles answered, "I've nearly finished." He walked into the men's ward carrying a urinal covered with a cloth.

Carmichael finished writing the report. She was longing to go outside the wards and listen at the lift but thought it was better not. She'd never seen the bottom of the lift because the lift itself of course always obscured it. There would be no one down in the basement at this time of night. She wondered whether they were dead or injured, just as she wondered about the cats. She really didn't mind about Jane and Doug; they had made her cats suffer and it would be right and proper if they suffered.

After giving her meticulous report to the Staff Nurse who was on duty that night she left her wards, made her way to the changing-room, changed almost mechanically, left the hospital saying a calm "Good night" to the telephonist, who was off at nine, got into her car and started to drive along the road towards her cottage.

Half-way there she felt she couldn't go home. She could not stand the emptiness of the cottage, couldn't stand what was left of the vandalism, couldn't stand the cat-door that never opened. She just couldn't go home. Then she remembered Mrs. Bradshaw's address. She'd looked it up in the notes. She would go and look for the cat, the blind cat. Poor thing, how could it do anything for itself, find any food? How long had Mrs. Bradshaw been in hospital? Ten days. It was probably dead by now, but still she must go and look.

CHAPTER 31

Carmichael turned her car round and drove back through the town and out into the country again, looking for Meadow Lane and then Ashy cottages. There were three in a row and all but one was in darkness. Number two, Mrs. Bradshaw's, was in the middle. Why hadn't the neighbour whose light was on fed the cat? She stopped the car, opened the little gate rather like her own, went up the path and looked into Mrs. Bradshaw's window. She had a torch with her and as she peered in, aided by the light, she could see a vague outline of furniture. Everything was shut, all the windows. She beamed her torch around.

The cottage on the left-hand side of her was in darkness and looked almost derelict. The one on the other side was the one that had lights in the window.

She went back and walked up the path of number one, the lighted cottage. She knocked on the door. There was a raucous barking and the noise of children's voices. A harassed-looking woman came to the door.

"Yes?" she said.

"Mrs. Bradshaw lives next door to you, doesn't she?"

The woman nodded. "Yes, she's in hospital, though. Fell down and broke her hip. She's not dead, is she?"

"No, no, she's not dead. I come from the hospital. She's worried about her cat."

"Oh, that 'orrible thing. I won't 'ave it near the place. It's got no eyes. Well, it's got eyes but they're sort of . . . I dunno what's the matter with it. She should have had it put down. Our dog chases it away."

"I see. Has it chased it away lately?" asked Carmichael, her voice cold.

"No 'e 'asn't. It 'asn't bin round since she's bin gone." A wail in the background, obviously from a baby, made her turn her head and she said to Carmichael abruptly, "I gotter go, it's the kid, see?" She closed the door, none too gently, almost in Carmichael's face before Carmichael had time to say that she was going round to the back of the cottages.

She went back to her car and turned her sidelights off, then walked to the back of the cottages, skirting the derelict one. The gardens, all three, seemed to run into the field behind them. All were completely untended. Ashy cottages looked as if it were due for demolition.

Carmichael walked through the long grass, calling as she went. She remembered the name of the cat—Fluffy. She went farther into the field still calling and as she did so the moon came out from behind some threatening clouds and lighted the scene. The field stretched either side of her and in front and all round her was country—hedges—trees. The cat must be dead, she was almost sure, but she went on. It was better out here in the field. There was nothing to distract her and her mind felt blank and peaceful.

She heard her own voice calling, calling as she had done for nights calling for Tibbles and Torty. Suddenly, almost to her horror or delight she wasn't sure, she heard herself calling "Harry, Harry." She stopped, put out her torch, and stood as if she had been struck. Harry? What was she doing calling Harry? She closed her eyes for a moment, shut her lids tight. Was she going mad? Well, nobody would care. She knew what the inside of a psychiatric hospital was like, she needn't worry. She opened her eyes again and started to call the cat but this time by its proper name. She was a long way from the cottages now, in a little clearing surrounded by a tangle of nettles and brambles lit up by her torch and the moon. Did she hear a miaow? She wasn't sure. She had put out the torch for a moment but now she switched it on and swung it round the bushes. The light was reflected back to her from the grey brambles. Suddenly there was something else, something white shone in the line of her torch, and out of the undergrowth wobbled Fluffy. Docilely the cat came towards Carmichael's voice, apparently not knowing where she was going. It staggered almost to Carmichael's feet and then suddenly collapsed.

Carmichael felt a swell of feeling, compassion, love. She picked up the animal. It was so light, so emaciated, she could feel every bone in its body. She held it in her arms, crooning to it, then bent down, picked up her torch, turned back, re-skirted the cottages. She didn't bother to go near them but went straight to the car, still crooning to the cat as she did so. She realized what she was saying and didn't contradict it or want to: "Harry, Harry, I'll look after you."

She opened the car door, placed the cat carefully on the passenger seat. It was alive, it was breathing, but it was too weak to move. She turned her car round and as she did so she noticed the front door of number one open and saw the woman peer out. Carmichael took no notice of her. She drove slowly along Meadow Lane, out into the main road, back through the town, and out to her own home.

Once the car was in the garage, she carried the cat carefully into the cottage. As she unlocked the door she prayed they would be there—the two cats—waiting for her, but they were not. The cottage was silent. Carmichael turned and locked the front door firmly behind her, then carried the cat through into the kitchen. She took a towel that was hanging on the door, spread it out on the draining-board, and laid the emaciated animal on it. It was, as Mrs. Bradshaw had said, half tabby and half white. The eyes looked up at her as she spoke, but they seemed sightless and clouded. One eye looked smaller than the other, as if the cat had had an injury to it. The sphere of the eye was a sphere no longer.

She got out milk, put a small amount in a saucepan in order to heat it just enough to take the chill off, then put it in a saucer and placed it in front of the cat, gently guiding its mouth, wetting its lips with her finger which she had dipped in the milk. It immediately started to lap, at first languidly, then tried to rise to its feet more comfortably. Carmichael helped it up and held it while it finished the milk.

A feeling of warmth and comfort flooded over Carmichael. She knew that she was still calling the cat Harry. She must not give it too much to eat—a tiny bit of food later. If she gave it too much, she might kill it. She poured a tiny drop more milk into the saucer, and the cat lapped that avidly, licking its lips. Could it be possible? She bent nearer, gently stroking it. Yes, it was purring. They were so nice, cats, so much nicer than people.

Carmichael moved away to put the saucer in the sink, and the cat immediately miaowed as if it knew she was not there. It would be a problem, she thought, but she would make the cat used to the cottage; after all, she'd got used to Mrs. Bradshaw's home. She thought again of Harry and his dislike of being helped, but this creature wouldn't dislike it, it would thank her, it would love her.

A slight noise made her turn. The cat-door was swinging very slightly. It must be the wind, she thought dully. As she watched it, suddenly a tabby head thrust its way through the opening and the usual quick motion followed so that the tail wouldn't be caught. The flap swung back again. The cat-door opened again. There they were, Tibbles and Torty. Carmichael could hardly believe it. She bent down. It was too much. As they started to rub round her, joyfully she burst into tears, forgetting Fluffy on the draining-board. She smoothed her hand over each of them in turn. They didn't seem to be injured in any way. They were thinner but otherwise all right. She got up, took a tin of cat food from the cupboard, and put a plateful down in front of each of them. They started to gnaw at it. Tibbles looked up at her in the middle of eating, saw Fluffy, and gave a quick, low hiss. Carmichael smiled for the first time in—how long?

"Now, Tibbles," she said, "that's Harry. She's come to stay with us and you're to be nice to her because she can't see." She gave a little grimace and then amended the name, "Harriet can't see." She stroked the top of the blind cat's head and then almost laughed. The name Harriet was acceptable, she thought.

"Do you remember Harry and how you sat on his knee?"

Tibbles obviously thought that for the moment food was more important than the intruder or the memories, so she went back to the food.

The telephone rang. For the moment Carmichael was worried whether it was the hospital. Had they found them alive? She had almost forgotten. Before she answered the phone she let it ring on, picking up the blind cat in her arms. She must find a box for it, put it in her little spare room for the night. She would give it some more food before that. She carried Harriet across to the phone. The cat lay on her knee, and Carmichael sat down by her little telephone table and picked up the receiver. She realized she was trembling again and feeling slightly sick. What was on the other end of the phone, what were they going to say? Two dead bodies had been found at the bottom of the lift shaft? It was not the hospital at all, it was Mrs. Sampson.

"Sister Carmichael," she said, "I just rang to see if you would come to bingo tomorrow. I thought it would take you out of yourself."

"They're back, my cats, they're back. They came back this evening. You must come in and see them, Mrs. Sampson, and bring your friend. You've been so kind."

"Oh, I am glad. I thought somehow they'd come back," answered Mrs. Sampson. It was a direct contradiction to what she had said before, and it steadied Carmichael.

"Yes, they've come back," she said and put down the receiver. As she did so she remembered that she'd quite forgotten to answer Mrs. Sampson's invitation to bingo, but then of course she didn't want to go. That game of chance wasn't her cup of tea. She looked down at the cat on her lap—she seemed completely relaxed now.

"We'll find you a bed and a blanket and get you comfortable for the night. Yes, you can have something to eat before you go to sleep," she said, and as if in answer to the cat's plaintive miaow—almost a silent miaow compared to the other two—Carmichael went on, "Yes, you can have a little more to eat before you go to bed." To her surprise the cat jumped off her lap and rubbed itself against her legs.

"Can you see a little, Harriet?" Carmichael asked, and as if in answer the cat looked up at her. "I'm glad if you can. It doesn't matter if you can see me and what I look like. You won't mind . . . It was only Harry . . ."

CHAPTER 32

Carmichael waked at her usual six o'clock. She liked to be up early to give herself plenty of time to do her few chores before she set out to the hospital, and she liked to get up early even when she was off duty.

Last night she had slept well and her two beloved cats had slept on the foot of her bed. Every time she had stirred during the night she had moved gently so as not to disturb them, and she had heard their reassuring purrs. It was unusual for them to sleep there, but she supposed, or liked to suppose, that their time away from her had been spent wanting her. It was a nice feeling.

She put on her dressing-gown and they both followed her downstairs, ready for their breakfast. She gave them their two plates of fish, opened the back door, and unlocked the little cat-flap, which she had bolted last night—not her usual procedure, but somehow she had felt apprehensive about their going out again. Tonight would be different.

Outside her back door there were a few rough flagstones. It was no longer raining and the sun was coming out. She moved the plates of fish out onto the flagstones and the two cats started eating.

Then Carmichael went up to the spare room, opening the door carefully, noiselessly. She didn't want to make the cat jump because, after all, she was like Harry, vulnerable to sudden noises.

The cat was no longer lying on its side in the lethargic way it had last night. It was curled up in a ball and raised its head as she approached the box. The two milky eyes looked up at her, one half-closed. Carmichael ran her hand over the thin body and dislodged two or three burs from its coat. She took the cat downstairs in her arms and into the garden, to one of the small flower beds she had made near the door. The flowers were dying, but the earth was still soft, and as she placed the cat on it, it stood upright, smelled the earth, then dug a hole and sat, its tail quivering slightly as it made itself comfortable. She watched it and, as it stood up and started to cover the patch, Carmichael's heart swelled with compassion. She fed it and it ate eagerly.

Carmichael closed the kitchen door. Her cats usually stayed out in the morning if it was sunny, and the sun had now risen and was warming the flagstones outside her back door. She took Fluffy—Harriet—upstairs again, put her back in the spare room, and shut the door. Then she had her bath and dressed and was ready for work. So far, so good, she thought.

She locked the back door, left open the cat-flap, went out of her front door and locked it. When she got the car out, there was no feeling of apprehension, no feeling that "they" might come back and wreck her little cottage again or injure the cats. No. She smiled to herself and wondered whether there would be an uproar when she got to the hospital. Would they tell her about the terrible thing that had happened?

She drove along in the early morning sunlight feeling a pleasant anticipation not in the least laced with worry.

When she arrived on her ward to receive the report from the night Staff Nurse, she was greeted by a barrage of remarks. The girl stood in her office as Carmichael sat down ready to listen to her, her finger in the report book but not yet reading from it. She had so much to tell she was bursting with news. Carmichael did not stop her, although normally she would have said, "Let's get on with the report, please, I'll hear the gossip later," but this morning she wanted to know what had happened.

"Oh, Sister, what a night! You've no idea . . ." Staff Nurse began.

Carmichael looked up at her. "Well, what—what happened?"

"To start with, Mr. Perkins fell out of bed and bruised his ribs. I think he'll have to be X-rayed."

"Surely that's part of the report, is it not, Staff Nurse?" said Carmichael.

"Yes, I know. I'll tell you about it in report. It's just that I want you to know the kind of night we've had. That was the first thing. Then Mrs. Bradshaw started about eleven-thirty. She went on all night. She was so noisy, kept trying to get out of bed. I had to get Dr. Patel up, so then I told him while he was here that Mr. Perkins had fallen out of bed."

"This is still the report, Staff Nurse," said Carmichael impatiently.

"Sister, I know I'm going on a bit, but wait till I tell you. That's not the important part."

"I'm sure it isn't," muttered Carmichael half to herself, grimly.

"Then we had a hip in, an old lady of ninety-four—Oh, by the way, the lift is mended. The men made a lot of noise and that didn't help the patients."

"Staff Nurse, will you either give me the report or tell me what it is that is so important," said Carmichael, who could wait no longer.

"Well, it was Nurse Andrews from Casualty. She's not very senior, but she brought this lady up in the lift. By the time she got up here, Sister, she was in hysterics, saying the lift was haunted. She said she'd heard moans—I ask you. I said it was the lady on the trolley, but Nurse Andrews would have that it wasn't. I couldn't do anything with her. She said it was the grey lady—you know, Sister, the one who is supposed to haunt this hospital. You're supposed to see her when somebody is going to die."

Carmichael tried to stem this flood. "Yes, every hospital I've been in has a grey lady," she said crisply. "Go on. What happened next?"

"Bill the porter was with her, and you know how deaf he is. Anyway, we got the old lady to bed—at least the porter and I did. Nurse Andrews didn't want to go back to Casualty. She wouldn't go downstairs. I had to give her some of the ward's brandy. To satisfy her, I went and got in the lift, Sister, and listened and I thought I heard something. It sounded ever so low and it could have been anything—the wind—only there wasn't any wind last night. In the end, I said I couldn't hear anything. We thought we'd pacified Nurse Andrews, and then she fainted! It was awful, Sister, it really was. It's bad enough having to look after the patients, isn't it, without having to look after the nurses. Anyway, Night Superintendent sent her off duty, but the porter had to go with her over to the Nurses' Home. I can tell you, Sister, I've never seen a nurse in such a state. I said to her, "You won't make much of a nurse at this rate," but I must admit I began to expect the grey lady to walk through those swing-doors." The Staff Nurse tittered nervously.

"I'll have the report now, Nurse."

Staff Nurse Munro slumped down in the chair beside Carmichael and began to read from the top of the page. As she droned on, Carmichael noticed that her hands, which she had clasped together as she listened to the Staff Nurse, were sweating. She took a tissue from the drawer and rubbed her palms gently.

"Mrs. Jones—comfortable night; Mrs. English—some pain in right knee, bandage loosened; Mrs. Freeman complained of sore heels . . ." It went on, a somewhat normal report, through the women's ward and the men's, with all the various highlights included—Mrs. Bradshaw and Mr. Perkins and, of course, the new admission, Mrs. Clayton—another hip.

"Leo Kalinsky—a comfortable night. Has slept all night. Not disturbed by the furore." He would, thought Carmichael, and she smiled to herself all the time his report was being read.

"And that's all, Sister," said Staff Nurse Munro, heaving a great sigh and closing the report book with a bang that made Carmichael frown. "I just hope I have a quieter night tonight."

"I hope so too," said Carmichael pleasantly. She had let the Staff Nurse talk far more than she would have done normally, merely because she wanted news of the two at the bottom of the shaft, and she had got it. Not quite what she had expected, but at least she knew that one of them had still been alive last night.

"Has anyone used the lift this morning? Has anyone heard any more of these strange sounds?" she asked.

"No, of course not, Sister. Yes, the lift has been going up and down as usual. It's different in the daylight, isn't it? I mean, you can imagine things at night, and Nurse Andrews has been on nights sometime. She's a bit timid, you know." Staff Nurse Munro laughed and her dusky face broke into a smile showing her white, even teeth. Carmichael nodded.

"Thank you, Staff Nurse," she said briskly, getting up. "You're on tonight?"

"Yes, Sister. Two more nights," she said cheerfully, and she picked up her coat and voluminous holdall from the floor near the office door and gave Carmichael a cherry "Good night, Sister."

CHAPTER 33

Carmichael stood for a moment or two tapping her Biro on her teeth. As she did so Geoffrey Miles went by.

"Great doings in the night. Ghastly moans and tappings, not to speak of everybody falling out of bed." He laughed genially and Carmichael half-smiled back.

"Hardly everybody falling out of bed, Staff Nurse," she said.

"Well, old Mrs. Bradshaw trying to get over her cot sides, and then Mr. Perkins—I'm surprised at him, I thought he was all right. Shall I put cot sides up for him too?"

"No, I don't think so. I think he probably got out of bed and was a bit muddled just because it was in the night. Leave it for the moment but tell the nurses to keep an eye on him."

Miles nodded and went on to the men's ward.

Carmichael stood a little longer watching her nurses flit to and fro, doing their morning duties. She picked up the bundle of mail from her desk and went as usual to distribute it and have a word with her patients.

Usually she went first to the men's ward, but this morning she chose to do otherwise and made her way towards the women's ward. She stopped by each bed, asking the patient how she felt, noting perhaps something that needed doing by one of the junior nurses or the orderly. Some complained that they had not slept a wink because of the noise, some demanding more sleeping pills. Some complained of constipation. It was the usual morning round. Carmichael arrived eventually at the bed nearest the door where they had put Mrs. Bradshaw. The old lady was sitting up and, as usually happened in the morning, she looked and sounded perfectly lucid.

"Good morning, Sister Carmichael," she said.

"Good morning, Mrs. Bradshaw, I want to talk to you."

There was no letter for Mrs. Bradshaw, there rarely was. Carmichael went and sat on the locker beside her bed, an unusual procedure for her. The old lady looked at her inquiringly and spoke in a rather quavery, querulous voice:

"I've been naughty, haven't I? At night, I mean. I don't know I do it, Sister. I hear somebody crying out and look round to see who it is and find it's me. Funny, isn't it?"

"No, it's just that you're worried and troubled, Mrs. Bradshaw. That's what I think," Carmichael said.

"I am. You're right there. I'm worried about Fluff. Ow, she's dead, I know, out of her misery, I suppose, but how miserable it must have been with me not there."

Suddenly the old lady put her brown-spotted hand over her eyes and down her cheek rolled big tears.

Carmichael gently pulled the old lady's hands down from her face and held them firmly between her own. "Mrs. Bradshaw, now listen to me carefully." She gazed straight into the old lady's face and the woman's wet eyes looked back at her. "I went to your cottage last night and I found Fluffy and she's alive, very thin and very weak, but she came to me." The old lady's mouth dropped open and she was about to say something, but Carmichael stopped her and went on, "I picked her up and took her home to my cottage. Then I fed her—only a little, because you mustn't give them too much when they've been"—she was going to say starving, but she thought it might upset the old woman, so she amended it—"without food for some time. I'll look after her until you go home." In her heart Carmichael knew the old lady would probably never go home to that derelict cottage, never, but for the moment . . .

"Oh, you've found her. But is it Fluffy? I mean . . ."

"She's tabby and white and blind."

"That's Fluffy," said the old lady. Her eyes brightened, her whole demeanour changed. She winced as she moved and her hip hurt her, but only for a second. Then she smiled.

"You're an angel, Sister, that's what you are, an angel. I'll never carry on again like I did last night. I felt all the time that

I just wanted to get up and try and find her, and I think that's why I make all these noises and try to get out of bed."

"I know it is too," said Carmichael. "So now there's no need. You can sleep all night because that's what Fluffy is doing. I made her a bed out of a carton and she got up this morning and stretched and yawned."

"She does, she does." The old lady clapped her hands together and then grabbed Carmichael's. Carmichael stood up. "You're an angel Sister from heaven, that's what you are." She turned to the old lady in the bed next to her. "She's an angel, that's what she is." The patient in the next bed turned up her deaf-aid, but it was too late, she hadn't caught what Mrs. Bradshaw had said, so she went back to reading her newspaper.

Carmichael left Mrs. Bradshaw's bedside, a warm glow suffusing her body. It was wonderful to see a patient helped, worry taken away from her. She felt that her nursing training was so justified, so right, and she had removed three people who might have injured it—Sampson with his talk of strikes and industrial action and those two terrible hooligans who might have gone and vandalized someone else's cottage, injured someone else's animals, cut a patient's extension—they were capable of anything. She was the one to deal out justice, not a stupid magistrate, who would just fine them or give them six months suspended sentence for beating up an old lady. No, she was the one, she was the one.

As she walked out of the women's ward her back was straight and her head was held high. She felt so much better, all her depression had gone. She was not going back into a psychiatric ward, never again. Soon, soon she would get promoted. They would see what kind of character she had. She stood no nonsense from anybody. She thought of Nurse Andrews. She'd once had her on the ward. A nice child, she thought, but impressionable, given to . . . well . . . who would believe her? Grey lady indeed, that moaning in the lift. It was lucky the porter had been slightly deaf. Still, that was her luck—holding, wasn't it? It was a good thing, and something she was used to.

Carmichael spent the morning supervising and teaching her nurses conscientiously. The clinical tutor came round and Carmichael withdrew into her own office. She didn't altogether trust the clinical Sister to teach her nurses as well as she, Carmichael, did, but then it was a post and it was recognized and she had to let the Sister have her way with her juniors. She did not approve of the way she let them call her "Pat," though, but even that couldn't ruffle Carmichael this morning. She felt all-powerful. Carmichael, Nursing Officer—that's what she would soon be.

Mr. Dalby's round this morning. Carmichael remembered that bad round she'd had with him some time ago. She grimaced and summoned the nurse who had handed her the wrong notes. She was determined to make sure it didn't happen again.

"Nurse, we will not have a repeat of your performance when Mr. Dalby was here a few weeks ago. You remember? I want everything to go perfectly, you understand? Please check the name on the notes and check it with the patient's headboard before you hand it to me even if you think you know the patient well. Right?"

The nurse nodded.

"Yes, Sister. I'm ever so sorry about that. I'll be careful this time, Sister, I really will."

Carmichael dismissed her and got on the phone to Dr. Patel. She'd better get Mr. Perkins squared up before the round.

A nurse looked into her office. "Mrs. Bradshaw, Sister, they had a bad night with her, so they say. Perhaps when Dr. Patel comes to see Mr. Perkins . . . He is coming, isn't he?" Carmichael nodded. "Do you think we could get her written up for some more sedatives? She is a trial, really she is, and she won't eat, either."

Carmichael looked at the nurse, then said, much to the nurse's surprise, "Sit down, Nurse, I want to talk to you."

Guardian Angel

The nurse sat primly on the other chair in Sister's office and looked demurely at Carmichael.

"Patients sometimes have home troubles we know nothing about."

"But Mrs. Bradshaw lives all by herself. She hasn't got any relatives to have trouble with. I don't see why she should . . ."

"She had problems at her home, a bad problem, and I have sorted it out for her."

"I thought the social worker . . ."

"A social worker is not always as capable of doing these things as we are led to believe, as my past experience has shown me," said Carmichael with some feeling. "So listen to the patient. Don't just think that she's moaning and groaning because she's senile. See if what she says is about a trouble that can be remedied. The social workers, you know, are not likely to be here in the middle of the night to listen to her."

"No, Sister Carmichael."

"I don't think we shall have much more trouble with Mrs. Bradshaw now."

"But I thought you . . . Yes, after all, it might be my grandmother, mightn't it?"

Carmichael looked at the young nurse. She was not pretty, her sandy hair was wispy rather like her own. She felt a sudden comradeship with her which she hastened to suppress.

"Yes, indeed," she said and dismissed the nurse with a nod of her head. The nurse got up and left Carmichael's office. Carmichael gazed after her for a long time and thought of little Marie, the battered baby, then dismissed the thought. That was in the past.

She felt complacent. The grey lady crossed her mind again and she smiled a little. She felt, for the moment, rather at one with the grey lady.

Carmichael stood at the same place at the ward door waiting for Mr. Dalby. She looked at her watch—precisely on time. The nurse with the note trolley stood beside her. Carmichael had given her another admonishing look and the nurse was geared ready to do everything correctly. Carmichael heard the whole orthopaedic circus mounting the stairs. No lift for them.

"Good morning, Sister Carmichael. All ready for me, I hope," Mr. Dalby said as he always did as he walked through the swing-doors, holding them open for the secretary, who followed him.

"Of course, sir," Carmichael answered.

"I see the lift is mended. Thank goodness for that. I thought disruption was going to be the order of the day." He turned to Mr. Harris, who was just behind the secretary. "They're putting in the new lift in a week, I hear. That little hiccup with the old one, I think, has speeded them up, so that's a good thing."

Mr. Harris nodded. They walked forward into the ward, Carmichael following them, determined not to let her thoughts stray, for they had slightly at the words "in a week." One week . . . Oh, well . . .

The round went off without a hitch. Miss O'Donoghue did not appear, much to Carmichael's relief. All the correct notes were handed to her, and they walked to the door that led out to the stairs.

"You've done well with that old Mrs. Bradshaw. She's calmed down a bit this morning. She was quite lucid with me today, chatting away. She's a nice old soul. Obviously you're very popular with her, Sister." He looked benignly at Carmichael.

It was obvious that the house officer was going to say something, but Carmichael's look quieted him as she answered the orthopaedic surgeon:

"Yes, sir, she's improved a lot, but they do sometimes if one tries to understand and find out if there's anything troubling them."

"Yes, indeed, yes, indeed, one often wonders whether the— the . . ." Mr. Dalby tailed off in mid-sentence and turned again to Mr. Harris. "That new fractured hip will have to be done this evening. Can you manage that all right without me? I'd rather you did if you could. It looks fairly simple."

"Yes, sir, of course, of course."

It was also obvious that Mr. Harris did not like the words "fairly simple."

They started down the stairs and Carmichael watched them. Near the top Mr. Dalby turned and raised his hand.

"I'm sorry, Sister Carmichael, I forgot to thank you. You run your ward excellently, Sister."

Carmichael flushed, then went and settled herself back into the routine. She didn't think about what lay at the foot of the lift, why should she? Something would happen . . . someone would discover them, of course, maybe before the new lift was put in. It really didn't matter. No suspicion would fall on her, it never did. It was almost amusing, really.

She took her coat from the back of the office door, ready to go to the dining-room to lunch. As she was about to leave the office her most junior nurse passed her, hesitated, and then came back.

"Yes, Nurse, what is it?" Carmichael asked.

"Sister, is there such a thing as the grey lady?" she asked.

Carmichael looked at her levelly as she answered. "Oh, yes, Nurse," she said, "I think there may well be."

The nurse looked back at her, her eyes wide. "Oh, thank you, Sister," she said and scuttled away, and Carmichael thought of the grey mufti dress hanging in the cupboard downstairs which she would change into tonight, and she smiled even more broadly.

At that moment the swing-doors opened and Miss O'Donoghue walked in, a most unusual time for her to come. She caught Carmichael's smile.

"You're looking more cheerful. I think you've borne up under all this marvellously, Sister, I really do." Her blue eyes looking at Carmichael were sincere and Carmichael replied:

"One must carry on, Miss O'Donoghue. The patients come first, don't they? One's own troubles, well . . ."

"Two bits of good news. I came to collect you to go down to lunch. The lift is going to be put in on Saturday. They're going to work over the week-end. Of course, it will take a long time, but that'll help."

Carmichael nodded her head but did not answer.

"Want to know the other bit of good news? It might affect you." Miss O'Donoghue's eyes sparkled and a mischievous smile played round her mouth. "I'm getting married, and we're off to Australia. What about that, then? My job will be going. Think you'll put in for it? You stand as good a chance as any—Sister Hill doesn't want it."

"I see." Carmichael paused, her coat still in her hand. Everything seemed to be going her way. That was nice. "Thank you for telling me. I certainly will put in for it. You will remember I was—"

"I know. You've had experience at the job. That's why I thought you'd stand a good chance. Of course, they may appoint someone from outside . . . Still, nothing venture, nothing win, eh?"

"No, indeed," said Carmichael, following her Nursing Officer through the swing-doors.

As they walked down the stairs, Miss O'Donoghue continued to chatter, but Carmichael's thoughts were elsewhere. Saturday . . . So they'd find them on Saturday, she thought. She wondered if cannabis showed in a post-mortem, whether they'd find out that they'd been smoking hash, or, indeed, if they took anything else. She wouldn't be surprised if they did. She wondered if the two of them lived together. Probably. That would account for there being no outcry from the girl's parents. She probably made a habit of living away from home when she felt like it. Yes, it was all fitting in very nicely. The police would be called in, of course, but Carmichael had dealt with that kind of situation before.

"You're not listening to a word I say," said Miss O'Donoghue as they arrived at the dining-room.

"No, I'm sorry. I was miles away—well, not miles, but rather deep in thought."

Carmichael again, rather to her own astonishment, smiled more broadly than ever, and the two of them made their way across the dining-room to lunch.

ANTHEA COHEN trained as a nurse at Leicester Royal Infirmary. For the past twenty-five years she has worked, on and off, in hospitals and as a private nurse. She has written on medicine and hospital life, been a columnist for *Nursing Mirror*, and has contributed regularly to *World Medicine*. She has published innumerable short stories and is a popular author of books for the teenage market in the United States. *Guardian Angel* is her fourth novel for the Crime Club.